Infectious Disease Specialists
Hunting Down Disease

Edward Willett

Enslow Publishing
101 W. 23rd Street
Suite 240
New York, NY 10011
USA
enslow.com

Published in 2016 by Enslow Publishing, LLC
101 W. 23rd Street, Suite 240, New York, NY 10011

Copyright © 2016 by Edward Willett

All rights reserved.

No part of this book may be reproduced by any means without the written permission of the publisher.

Cataloging-in-Publication Data
Willett, Edward.
Infectious disease specialists: hunting down disease / by Edward Willett.
p. cm. — (Extreme science careers)
Includes bibliographical references and index.
ISBN 978-0-7660-6970-1 (library binding)
1. Epidemiology — Juvenile literature. 2. Epidemiologists — Juvenile literature.
I. Willett, Edward, 1959-. II. Title.
RA653.5 W58 2016
614.4—d23

Printed in the United States of America

To Our Readers: We have done our best to make sure all Web site addresses in this book were active and appropriate when we went to press. However, the author and the publisher have no control over and assume no liability for the material available on those Web sites or on any Web sites they may link to. Any comments or suggestions can be sent by e-mail to customerservice@enslow.com.

Portions of this book originally appeared in the book *Disease-Hunting Scientist: Careers Hunting Deadly Diseases*.

Photo Credits: Adam Pletts/Getty Images, p. 25; Andrej Vodolazhskyi/Shutterstock.com, pp. 3 (background); ©AP Images, pp. 9, 12, 21, 23, 37, 45, 79, 92, 94, 102; Borisoff/Shutterstock.com, p. 66; Bruce Dale/National Geographic/Getty Images, p. 11; BSIP/Getty Images, p. 49; BSIP/UIG/Getty Images, p. 6; Carlos E. Santa Maria/Shutterstock.com, p. 3 (scientist); CELLOU BINANI/AFP/Getty Images, p. 15; © Consortiu, for the Conservation Medicine/Wildlife Trust, pp. 106, 109, 111; Courtesy Jonathan Runstadler, pp.73, 76; Courtesy of the Everett Collection/alamy, p. 16; FLORENCE PANOUSSIAN/AFP/Getty Images, p. 90; jaddingt/Shutterstock.com (chapter heads throughout book) Jonathan Drake/Bloomberg via Getty Images, p. 36; Kathryn Scott Osler/The Denver Post via Getty Images, p. 83; leungchopan/Shutterstock.com, p. 68; M. Guerra, pp. 17, 18; Media for Medica/Getty Images, p. 88; Pete Nieson/Shutterstock.com, p. 77; PETER PARKS/AFP/GettyImages, p. 101; Pernille Bering/ Shutterstock.com, p. 30; Pierre-Yves Babelon/Shutterstock.com, p. 40; Photo by Laurie Richardson, pp. 53, 57, 62; pzAxe/Shutterstock.com, p. 113; Public Health Agency of Canada, pp. 34, 43, 86; Rich Carey/Shutterstock.com, p. 55; SAM YEH/AFP/Getty Images, p. 70; Spectacled flying fox (Pteropus conspicillatus)/Getty Images, p. 38; Stocktrek Images/Getty Images, p. 10; © Stephen Frink Collection / Alamy, p. 58; Tyler Hicks/Getty Images, p. 27; TONY KARUMBA/AFP/Getty Images, p. 29; Universal Images Group via Getty Images, p. 60; Volodymyr Goinyk/Shutterstock.com, p. 50; Warner Bros/Ronald Grant Archive/Alamy, p. 16; Wild Art/Shutterstock.com, p. 81; Werner Layer/Animals Animals - Earth Sciences, p. 104.

Cover Credits: Andrej Vodolazhskyi/Shutterstock.com (background); Carlos E. Santa Maria/Shutterstock.com (scientist).

Contents

1 Investigating Disease 7

2 Marta Guerra: Battling Ebola 13

3 James Strong: Science in a Space Suit 33

4 Laurie Richardson: Stalking the Coral Killer 51

5 Jonathan Runstadler: The Biology of Bird Flu 69

6 Lisa Fernando: An Outbreak of Marburg 85

7 Jonathan Epstein: Seeking the Source of SARS 99

Appendix: Infectious Disease Specialists: Jobs at a Glance 118

Chapter Notes 119

Glossary 122

Further Reading 124

Index 125

The influenza virus as seen with an electron microscope. Infectious disease scientists study why people get certain diseases and what can be done to stop those diseases from spreading.

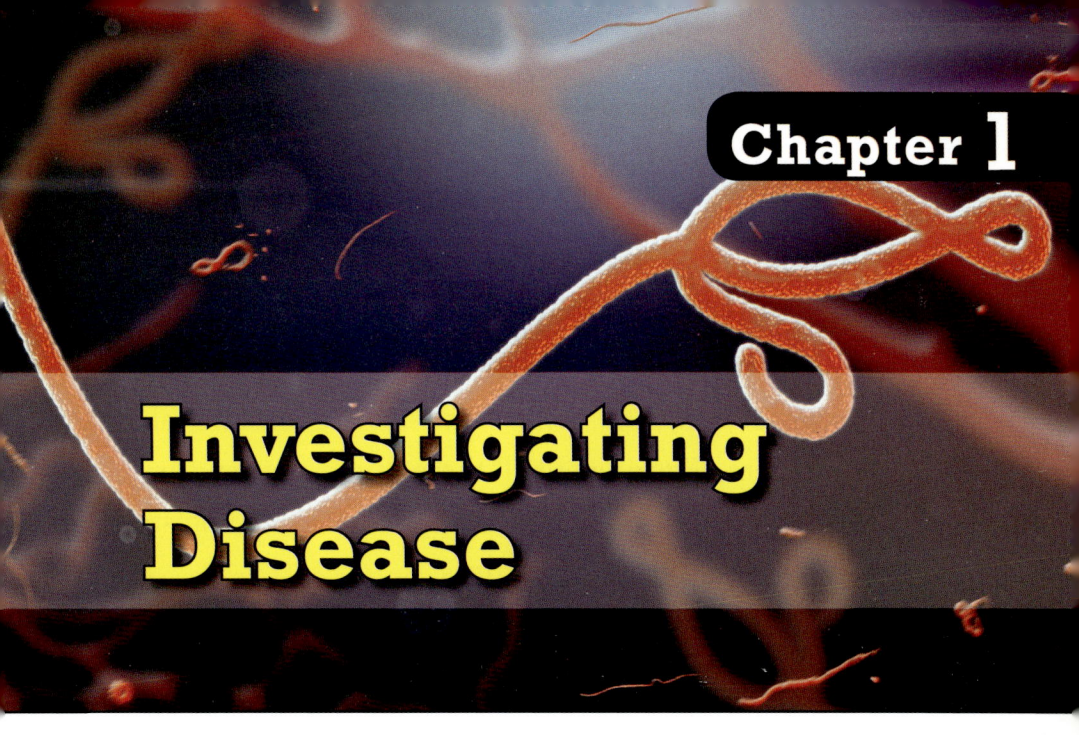

Chapter 1
Investigating Disease

If you've always thought that scientists spend all their time wearing white lab coats and either peering through microscopes or juggling test tubes, then you're about to have your eyes opened. The scientists you will read about in this book have spent plenty of time in the laboratory—but they've also done a few other things, like stringing mesh nets in Chinese caves to catch bats, rolling along darkened African roads hoping to avoid armed rebels, scuba-diving on coral reefs off the coast of Florida, and camping in the Alaskan wilderness (though admittedly not all at the same time).

You have to admit it all sounds pretty extreme. And those are just some of the things these scientists have done while investigating diseases. You may have heard of some of these diseases, such as Ebola. Other diseases, such as black band disease, are probably new to you.

Infectious Disease Specialists

While some of the scientists in this book are medical doctors and others are biologists or veterinarians, almost all of them also call themselves epidemiologists. Epidemiology is the study of how often diseases affect different groups of people or animals, where different diseases develop, and why some people or animals develop them. Figuring out all these things is often very much like solving a mystery. That is why epidemiologists are often called "disease detectives."

More and more, the epidemiology of diseases in humans and the epidemiology of diseases in animals are linked. There is a good reason for this. According to one recent study, out of 1,415 viruses, bacteria, and parasites known to cause disease in humans, 61 percent are zoonotic. That means they can be transmitted between humans and animals. The same study indicates there are 175 disease-causing organisms that are considered "emerging," meaning the diseases they cause have only recently been identified. Of those new diseases, 75 percent are zoonotic.[1]

Some of the most dangerous new diseases began with animals. As people continue to move into areas of the earth where humans have not lived before, they will continue to drive animals out of their natural habitats. Animals that have had very little contact with humans before will now have more and more. That means that there are likely to be more emerging diseases making the jump from animals to humans. And since international

INVESTIGATING DISEASE

A scientist extracts frozen cells from ape and dog kidneys to be used in a possible vaccine for avian influenza.

Infectious Disease Specialists

Some disease scientists study deadly viruses like Ebola, shown here under a microscope.

air travel is so common, those emerging diseases can quickly spread around the world.

To protect human health, we need to know more about how these organisms cause disease in humans, how they jump from animals to humans, and how outbreaks of these diseases can be controlled.

Disease detectives also work with nonhuman diseases, such as the black band disease that is killing coral reefs. Diseases like this can have a devastating impact on the environment as a whole, harming not only the species directly affected but also all those that are linked to it within a particular habitat.

Disease detectives, in other words, have their work cut out for them. As you will see in this book, they are up to the task. To learn what they can about emerging diseases and help those affected by them, they will go to any lengths, depths, and heights . . . no matter how extreme.

INVESTIGATING DISEASE

A researcher removes a bat caught in a mist net for testing. This is one of the many possible jobs of a disease-fighting scientist.

The family of Ebola victim Emile Ouamouno. Emile was the first patient to contract Ebola in his village, which became ground zero for the worst Ebola epidemic in history.

Chapter 2

MARTA GUERRA

Battling Ebola

On December 6, 2013, a two-year old boy named Emile Ouamouno died in a small village in Guinea. The cause of death was Ebola hemorrhagic fever. He was the first person in his village to ever contract Ebola. By January, his three-year-old sister, his mother, and his grandmother had all died.

Though no one knew it at the time, it was the start of the largest Ebola epidemic in history, an epidemic which is continuing: As of February 25, 2015, there had been 23,729 suspected, probable and confirmed cases, 14,237 laboratory-confirmed cases, and 9,604 deaths across several West African countries.

Inspired by a Movie

Even before the current epidemic, Ebola had held a grip on the imagination of people around the world.

Infectious Disease Specialists

Ebola Hemorrhagic Fever

Ebola fever is a deadly disease that gets its name from the Ebola River near Yambuku, Democratic Republic of the Congo, Africa. That region was the site of the first recognized outbreak.

Ebola begins with influenza-like symptoms: fever, weakness, muscle pain, headache and sore throat. Eventually, vomiting, diarrhea, and rash develop. The kidneys and liver may stop functioning normally. In fatal cases, uncontrollable internal and external bleeding begins, resulting in the vomiting of blood, and bleeding from the eyes, ears, nose, and other body openings.

The disease is transmitted through direct contact with the blood or other bodily fluids (sweat, saliva, etc.) of the infected person or by contact with objects contaminated with infected bodily fluids. No airborne transmission of Ebola has ever been documented in humans.

Currently, there is no effective treatment for Ebola, although research continues into possible treatments and a vaccine seems imminent. The best doctors can do is treat the symptoms until the patient's own immune system can fight off the infection on its own—if it is able to. Treatment includes intravenous fluids that include electrolytes (sodium, potassium, and chloride) and oxygen; drugs to control fever, help the blood clot, and maintain blood pressure; and antibiotics to prevent secondary infections from bacteria.

Death occurs in 50 to 90 percent of cases. Why some people recover and others do not is not well understood, although Ebola victims who die have typically not developed a significant immune response to the virus.[1]

MARTA GUERRA: BATTLING EBOLA

In March 2015, a health worker prepares an Ebola vaccine for clinical trials in Guinea. Scientists believe a vaccine will be available to the public soon.

In the movie *Outbreak*, a kind of super-Ebola virus—which kills everyone who contracts it—arrives in the United States, carried by an infected African monkey. Researchers from the US Army Medical Research Institute for Infectious Diseases and the Centers for Disease Control and Prevention (CDC) have to figure out how to stop it. *Outbreak* came out in 1995—the same year that Marta Guerra was finishing her master's degree in public health.

Marta Guerra had grown up in Washington, D.C., exposed to a lot of different cultures. In high school she decided to become a veterinarian. She received her

Infectious Disease Specialists

The popular 1995 film *Outbreak*, starring Dustin Hoffman and Rene Russo, shed a light on infectious diseases with its story of scientists fighting a deadly pandemic.

MARTA GUERRA: BATTLING EBOLA

Marta Guerra's work in epidemiology sometimes takes her to faraway places. This photo was taken after she visited a health clinic in Ethiopia.

doctor of veterinary medicine degree from the University of Florida in 1985. While practicing as a vet, she says, she became very interested in zoonotic diseases—diseases that come from animals—and science education. "At some point I decided I would go back to school and do public health."[2]

And then she went to see *Outbreak*. "I was looking around for work, and I remember seeing that movie and thinking, 'Wow, that's what I want to do!'"

Fast-forward to November 2000. Dr. Guerra, now with a PhD in epidemiology and recently hired as an officer of the Epidemic Intelligence Service (EIS)

Infectious Disease Specialists

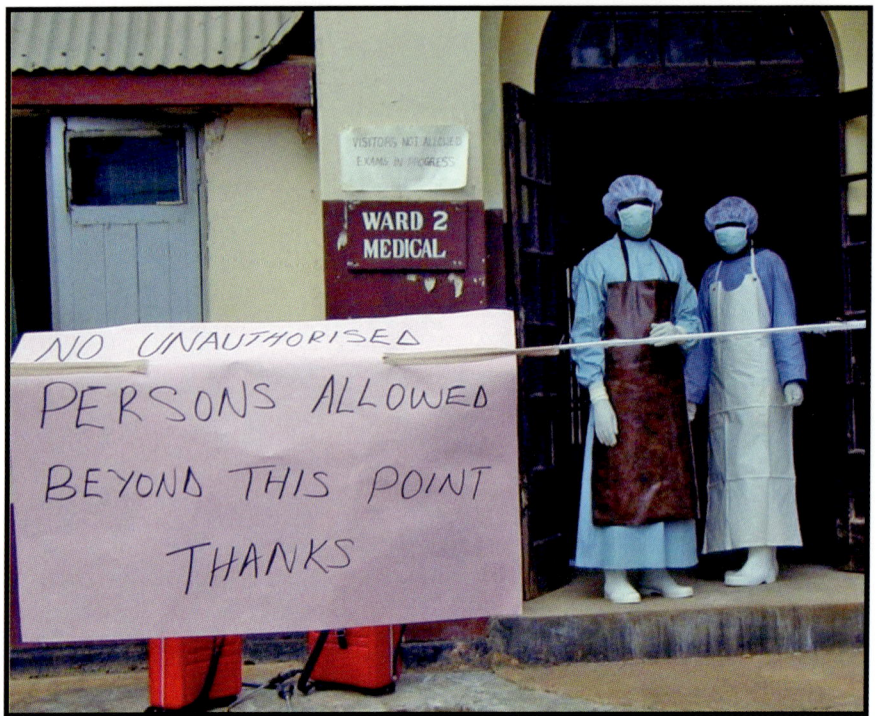

This photo was taken outside the hospital where Guerra helped review the medical records of Ebola patients.

program of the CDC, received orders to head out on her first international mission. She would be helping to study and combat an outbreak in Uganda, Africa, of Ebola virus—the very virus the disease in *Outbreak* was based upon. "It was very ironic," she says.

It was also unexpected. "I had done a couple of days of a domestic [in the United States] case investigation but I really did not expect to be asked to go on an international trip that early. Basically I heard rumors on a Tuesday and by Thursday we heard we were going— and leaving Sunday."

Leaving in a Hurry

The next couple of days were a whirlwind of preparation. That Friday, she headed to the health clinic to get all of the necessary vaccinations. "I think I received about five shots in one day to prepare," Guerra recalls. Arrangements also had to be made for her to travel on her personal passport, because she did not have an official passport—a special passport issued to employees of the United States assigned overseas. "Our embassy has to agree that you can come to the country, so there is a lot of paperwork involved," she says. And then there was all the equipment to assemble. She wanted to make sure she had plenty of personal protection equipment: gloves, booties, and masks.

Guerra flew to Africa with another, more experienced EIS officer, and two laboratory technicians. They joined five other team members from the CDC who were already in Lacor, Uganda, working in a laboratory set up at St. Mary's Hospital, a private hospital established by an Italian doctor. St. Mary's had much more advanced equipment than the local government-run hospital. It was already set up with the equipment Guerra and her colleagues needed, so the team was able to diagnose people in less than twenty-four hours.

Accurate diagnosis was important, she says, not only to identify people who had Ebola, but also to identify those who did not so that they could keep healthy people separate from the suspected Ebola patients.

Infectious Disease Specialists

Tracking the Spread

Guerra's work during the outbreak included tracking the spread of the disease, identifying those who had been exposed, and educating the public.

"Part of what we did was to try to organize the database, to make sure that we had everyone who was in the hospital listed, and that we had all of the contacts listed," she says. Every day Guerra and other doctors and volunteers would go to the government-run hospital and get the list of people who were newly admitted and newly diagnosed. "Then we would go out to the person's home and make a list of [his or her] contacts. Those contacts would have to be visited for twenty-one days. If there was anyone that appeared to be unhealthy or developing any kind of symptoms, then we would call . . . the hospital to bring an ambulance out," Guerra said.

In total, about 150 trained volunteers helped in this surveillance project. Over the course of the outbreak, 5,600 people who had been in contact with infected patients were identified and observed.

Another important component of Guerra's work was education, a process helped by the fact that, in Uganda, most of the people who have attended school understand English. Guerra and her team visited villages—some just small groups of huts placed close together—and announce the reason for their visit and what was happening. Guerra found that the locals "had amazing questions. Without having medical knowledge they were asking a lot of good questions as far as transmission and how to protect themselves."

Educating the Public

The Ugandan government, Guerra says, had done a wonderful job educating people about another deadly virus that plagues the region: HIV(human immunodeficiency virus), the virus that causes AIDS(acquired immunodeficieny syndrome). But the lessons learned regarding HIV actually made it harder to deal with Ebola.

A Red Cross medical officer gives local Ugandans information about the Ebola virus.

Infectious Disease Specialists

"HIV is very different," Guerra points out. "Once you are positive you stay positive, and most likely you are eventually going to die from it. So they transferred that concept into, 'OK, your test was positive for Ebola, therefore you're positive for Ebola and you're going to have it for the rest of your life.'"

She says it took a lot of work to get the people to understand the difference between HIV and Ebola. When you test positive for antibodies to HIV, it means you are infected with a disease that will most likely kill you and can be passed on to other people. But if you survive Ebola, you are no longer contagious and the antibodies in your body protect you from contracting the disease again. "It was sort of trying to tease out some very specific scientific concepts about immunology and then trying to explain it to them in terms they understood."

Because of what they'd learned about HIV, Guerra says, people thought that anyone with antibodies to Ebola was contagious and was dangerous to have around. As a result, survivors of the disease were being cast out from the villages, away from their families, with no food, because people feared sharing their food with Ebola survivors or letting them use their dishes.

It became an important part of the education process for Guerra to show others that touching and interacting with these survivors was not dangerous. "I would definitely go up and touch them, or try to show them that I was not scared to be around them." She would

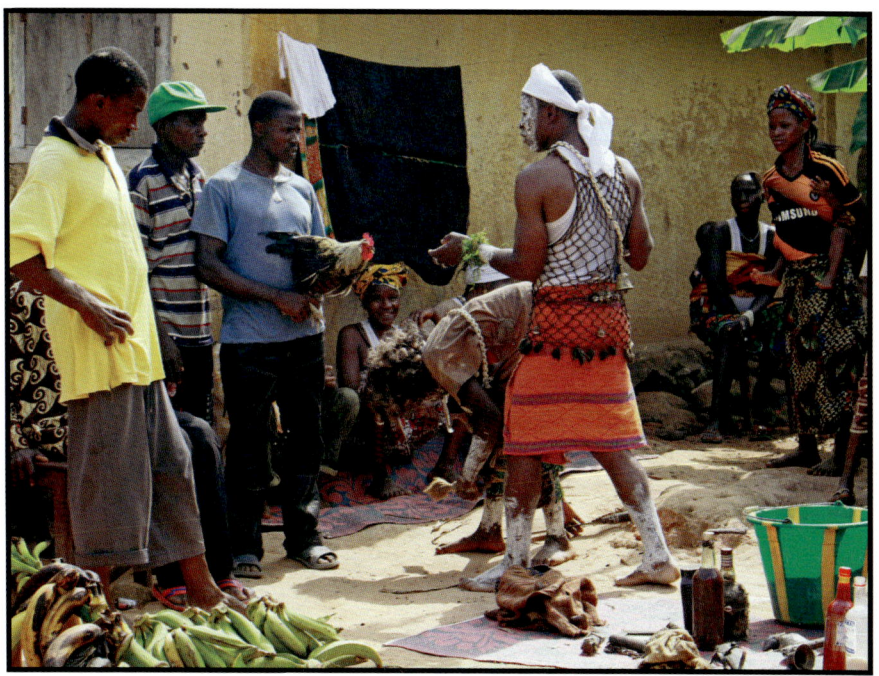

Many West Africans rely on traditional healers, like the ones seen here, during the 2015 Ebola outbreak, rather than medical doctors.

often give the survivors money so they could buy food or pots and pans and something to sleep on.

Another aspect of education was telling local residents that they had to go immediately to the hospital to get checked out if they experienced any flu-like symptoms. That was important, Guerra says, because it meant that those who were infected did not have time to transmit the virus to anyone else.

Most people in the area would first be cared for by family members when they became ill, Guerra explains. After that, they would probably turn to traditional healers. "They wouldn't necessarily go to a clinic,

> **Infectious Disease Specialists**

because there are usually very few of them and it would be a very far walk," Guerra says. That led to tragedies like the death of all four sisters in one family because they took care of each other as they fell ill one by one.

To avoid that, the team members urged the local people to go to a clinic as soon as they felt ill. "If it was malaria, then good, you got your treatment early and you'd be on your way to recovery," she would tell them. On the other hand, if it was Ebola, victims could quickly be isolated from their family, and supportive care could be started.

Only Worried Once

Despite the well-publicized deadliness of Ebola, Guerra says she was not particularly concerned about the risk of contracting the disease herself. "Because I was going as an epidemiologist, I didn't think I was going to be actually taking care of patients," she says. "My role was working with the local health department and all of the other international organizations that were there. Because I knew how to protect myself as far as wearing all the personal protection equipment, I wasn't nervous at that time."

But she did get concerned about being exposed on one visit to the home of an Ebola patient who had a little boy who was about two years old. "She was in the hospital at the time, and we were out checking her family. The little boy at first was very scared of me, but after three or four days he finally came up to me and gave me this big

MARTA GUERRA: BATTLING EBOLA

The Lord's Resistance Army rebels in Uganda were yet another danger faced by the Ebola workers.

hug around my legs, and I hugged him back. The next day we came out and the little boy was not there, and they said they had to take him to the hospital.

"[I was] thinking, 'Well, could it be Ebola?' Here I was in very close contact with him the day before."

Fortunately, for both Guerra and the little boy, his symptoms were due to malaria, not Ebola.

The researchers were more worried about people than viruses, Guerra recalls, "We were in the territory of the Lord's Resistance Army [a rebel group] in northern Uganda. A lot of people had been displaced up there, a lot of people kidnapped and killed, so there was a curfew. Every day we had to try to make sure we got home before

Infectious Disease Specialists

dark. When you are in these kinds of conditions you are working around the clock. It was very difficult to pack everything up and go home."

Guerra's scariest moments came one night when the team missed the curfew and had to drive home in the dark.

> *There are woods on either side. It's at night, and there is no streetlight. It's a dirt road, and unless there is a moon out, it is just pitch black. The headlights only go maybe ten or fifteen feet ahead of the car. By the time you see somebody they are quite close.*
>
> *It's just amazing how many people are traveling the roads, just walking, at night. A couple of times, you would come up, you would see some people in uniforms, and it was hard to tell whether they were soldiers from the Ugandan army or whether they could possibly be some of these rebels.*

There was reason to be concerned: Some scientists from South Africa came under fire from snipers during one trip into the war-torn north.

The hospital and the center of Lacor were considered safe, Guerra says, and most of the Ebola patients her team visited were close to the town, within about three miles (five kilometers). However, when they heard of a case farther north in one of the refugee camps, they needed a military escort to check it out.

"It was a very different atmosphere in the refugee camp. Everyone was very quiet and very suspicious. People were starting rumors that we wanted to take their blood in order to sell it, so we were not getting very much cooperation as far as drawing samples. Everybody just seemed very tense and very scared."

In the end, though, Guerra's team saw nothing of the Lord's Resistance Army. "I think they were also very scared of the Ebola outbreak," she says.

They had good reason to be frightened. The 2000 Ugandan outbreak killed 225 people before it was brought under control.

A CDC worker at St. Mary's Hospital in Uganda tests blood samples for the Ebola virus.

Infectious Disease Specialists

A Wonderful Experience

Guerra remained in Uganda for a month. Despite the deadliness of the disease and the danger from the rebels, she calls the experience "just wonderful."

"For people who like to do fairly exciting things, not just for the thrill of it but also to feel like you are actually helping people, it was a wonderful experience," she says.

There were scientific benefits as well. "Whenever these things happen, it is always a chance to learn more about the disease and how it spreads, so that hopefully the next time it comes up you can apply your preventive measures a little bit faster and better."

The Uganda outbreak was different from previous outbreaks of Ebola because of the fairly sophisticated laboratory equipment available to the doctors and researchers. Doctors had found that many of the people who seemed to recover (about half, in the Ugandan outbreak) were not recovering well. "They were not feeling like they were getting their energy back," Guerra says.

Thanks to the equipment available at St. Mary's Hospital, the CDC team was able to do some of the laboratory tests that are usually done in other hospitals around the world to diagnose problems.

What they found was the recovering patients had very low levels of the mineral potassium. Providing the patients with extra potassium was an easy and effective solution. "They almost looked like they came back to life, and they were able to recover and go home much

MARTA GUERRA: BATTLING EBOLA

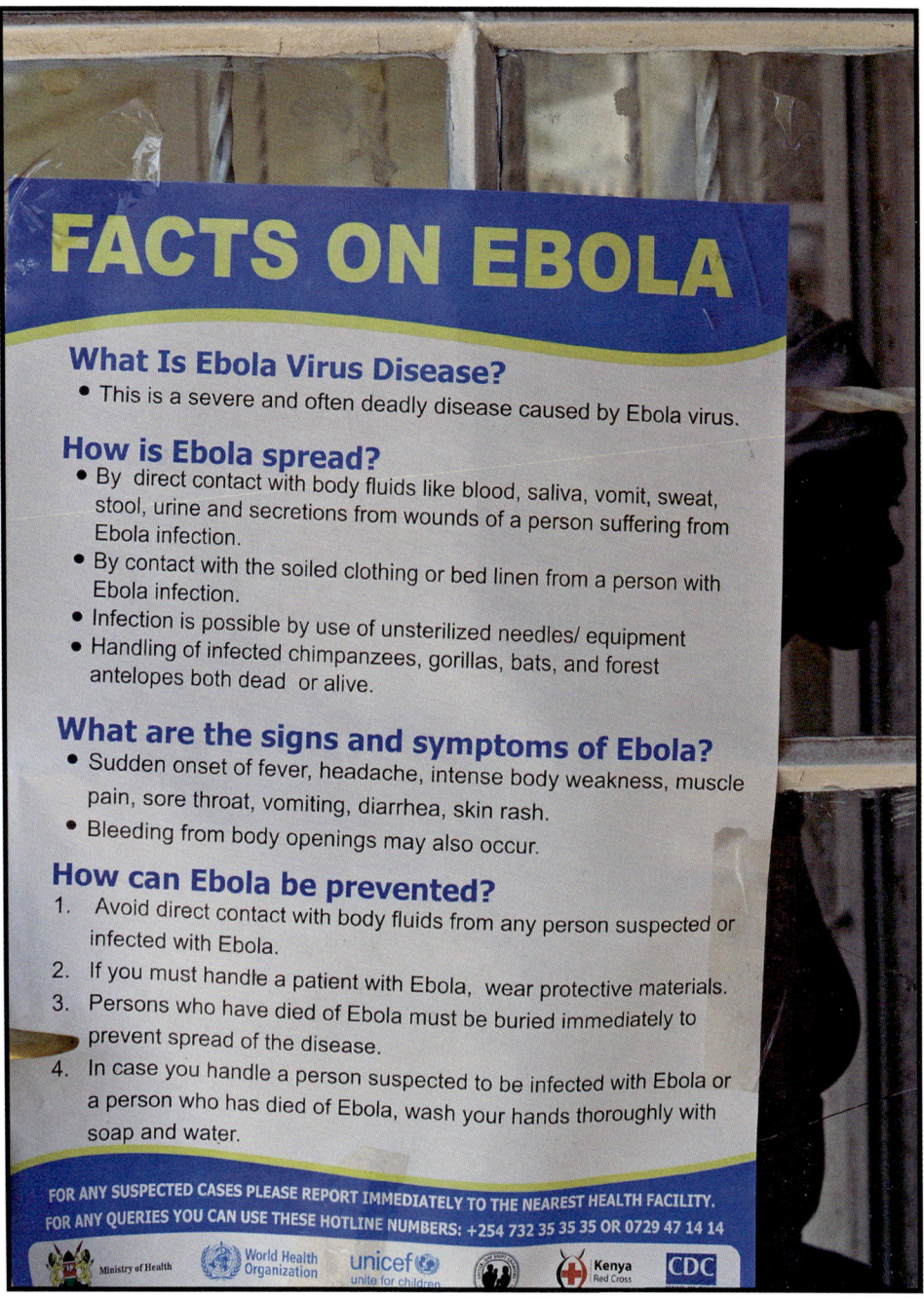

A patient walks behind a poster carrying information on prevention and handling of suspected Ebola cases at Mbagathi district hospital in 2014.

Infectious Disease Specialists

Epidemiologist Guerra says the focus of her work is not on individuals, but on populations like these Ugandans.

more quickly. That was something that we did not know beforehand. You always figure if you go through the acute phases of the disease and you survive you should be bouncing back quickly. It was interesting finding out that there are maybe other reasons why people are not."

Still Doing Her Part

Although the Ugandan outbreak happened a decade and a half ago, Guerra says the work she did then still reflects the work that scientists are doing today in the countries affected by the current epidemic. And she's been doing her part, as well.

"Everyone at CDC has been doing their part to volunteer for the response," she said. "I spent six weeks with the Unaffected Countries Team that was involved with preparation activities in countries bordering the affected countries. I traveled to Niger to be part of a WHO Preparedness Support Team for Ebola that evaluated the country's preparedness and ability to respond to an Ebola case."

There is always a need for more people to work in the field in outbreaks like the one in Uganda, Guerra says. Even though a lot of people think the work sounds very exciting, there are not many people who would actually be willing to go. "A lot of times you have difficulty recruiting people to go to work in these kinds of conditions," Guerra says.

She recommends that young people considering a career in epidemiology work toward some kind of health-professional degree. "It doesn't necessarily have to be medical," she says. "It could be dental, it could be veterinary, it could be a master's in public health or a PhD in epidemiology or some kind of laboratory science."

The important thing, she says, is to focus on dealing with populations—groups of people with something in common—as opposed to individuals. "You still have to learn the medicine at the individual level, but definitely look at diseases that are communicable [contagious] and

Infectious Disease Specialists

try to focus on types of professions that deal with people in larger populations."

Of course getting good grades in science and math classes is important, Guerra says, "but we always seem to forget that you need good communication skills. I still recommend doing well in English and being able to write well and having experience in communicating with others."

And not just in English, either. "Studying foreign languages is important," she adds. "We have a shortage of French speakers for the Ebola response."

It might also be worthwhile to rent the movie *Outbreak*, Guerra says. Of course it's not an entirely accurate portrayal of life as a disease detective, but "the value in those films is opening up the idea that there could be diseases out there that we still don't know—there's still so much about science that we don't know." And, she adds, there are "chances to go out there and help people who are in a very disadvantaged state… chances to go out there and do investigations."

Chapter 3

JAMES STRONG

Science in a Space Suit

Have you ever seen something like this in a movie?

There's a scientist—a beautiful scientist—battling a mysterious illness, racing the clock in a high-tech Level 4 laboratory, encased in a plastic suit to protect herself from the pathogen killing people right and left. She's made a breakthrough. She knows how to cure the disease! But then, a slip of the knife (or perhaps sabotage) and she's exposed to the very illness she's striving to cure. It's experimental—it may not work—but she decides she will be the first to try it. Fade out on either a happy ending or the end of the world, depending on what kind of movie it is.

But what is it like to work in a Level 4 laboratory in real life? Dr. James Strong knows. He's the head of the

Infectious Disease Specialists

The Level 4 suit goes on over a pair of surgical scrubs. An air hose is attached on the back to give the researcher clean air to breathe.

Diagnostics and Therapeutics Section of the Department of Special Pathogens at the National Microbiology Laboratory in Winnipeg, Canada. Most working days he spends at least a couple of hours in the lab. So how did Strong end up working in a lab that requires the most extreme safety measures possible?

Although he is a pediatrician (a medical doctor specializing in children) by training, Strong says he has also done work in virology, the study of viruses. While training to be a pediatrician, Strong was looking for a research focus when one of the infectious disease doctors suggested he speak to Heinz Feldmann, the chief of special pathogens at the National Microbiology Laboratory. "He said, 'Would you be interested in working on some of these more nasty pathogens like Ebola and Marburg?' and I thought, 'Yes!'" Strong recalls.[1]

Strong had always been interested in virology, an interest sparked in part by an outbreak of Ebola in Kikwit, Zaire, now known as the Democratic Republic of the Congo. The outbreak occurred in 1995, during Strong's medical training, and he was soon working with Feldmann to create a research program they could work on together.

Discovering Ebola's Hiding Place

Strong's research has focused on how the Ebola virus is transmitted from animals to humans. "One of the big 'holy grails' as far as Ebola and Marburg research is [concerned is] where does the virus hide between

Infectious Disease Specialists

The Four Levels of Containment[2]

Containment levels **refers** to the measures a laboratory uses to prevent the accidental escape of the bacteria or viruses scientists are researching there.

In a **Level 1 lab**, scientists work with microorganisms that do not cause disease in healthy adults. Two examples are *E. coli* (a kind of bacteria that can cause food poisoning, but isn't contagious) and infectious canine hepatitis virus, which makes dogs sick, but not humans. The only necessary protective measure is a sink for washing hands.

A **Level 2 lab** is used for research on disease-causing microorganisms that can be worked with safely in the open, provided there is no risk of splashing or spraying. Closed cabinets, splash shields, face protection, gowns, and gloves are used as needed. Examples of Level 2 microorganisms are those that cause measles, salmonella, and Hepatitis B.

Level 2 lab

Level 3 labs are where researchers work with microorganisms that can cause serious, potentially deadly infections that can be transmitted through breathing. In Level 3 labs all samples are handled inside closed, airtight cabinets. The lab itself usually has controlled access and the air going into and out of it is carefully filtered. Examples of Level 3 microorganisms are those that cause tuberculosis (an infectious disease that primarily attacks the lungs) and some forms of encephalitis (inflammation of the brain).

Level 3 lab

Finally, **Level 4 labs** are designed to enable researchers to work safely with dangerous and exotic samples that cause life-threatening diseases that can potentially be transmitted through the air, and for which no vaccine or effective treatment exists. The lab has its own ventilation system and nothing goes out of it—not air or waste materials—without being thoroughly decontaminated. Workers in Level 4 labs all wear "space suits" for which air comes from outside the lab. Examples of Level 4 microorganisms are the viruses that cause the Ebola and Marburg hemorrhagic fevers.

Infectious Disease Specialists

It has long been suspected, but not confirmed, that the fruit bat is the source of the Ebola virus.

outbreaks, or in other words what is the reservoir?" he says. A "reservoir" is a species of animal in which the virus may circulate without much effect. It does not cause serious illness until it jumps from the reservoir species to another species (such as humans) that is not adapted to it.

> *There's been a lot of suggestion that [the Ebola virus] is in [the] fruit bat species right now, but no one has ever been able to prove that in the field. We think that in the case of most of these Ebola outbreaks, a nonhuman primate—a monkey or a great ape—has been involved somewhere in the transmission to the human outbreak. What we don't know is how the primate is getting it.*

Those species suffer from Ebola even more than humans—their fatality rates are even higher—which makes it unlikely they are the reservoir species, Strong says. "They'd be killed off as quickly as we would. We would be a lousy reservoir species as well!"

Strong's current research interest is studying how the virus disrupts the body systems of the affected in order to better understand ways of treating these infectious diseases. These studies include cell cultures and animal models, as well as some studies on human patients during outbreaks that occur in African countries. This often requires travel to remote parts of Africa via planes, trucks, or even dugout canoe. "You have to be adaptable in this line of work," he says, "as the conditions where these viruses emerge are not always comfortable." His field research can take place in 100°F (38°C) heat,

Infectious Disease Specialists

Disease researchers like James Strong must sometimes visit remote areas of Africa to obtain samples to study.

JAMES STRONG: SCIENCE IN A SPACE SUIT

with 100 percent humidity, and involves traveling over rough to almost impassable roads, with mosquitoes, rats, and other pests in abundance in some of the areas where outbreaks occur. "The Level 4 lab is extremely comfortable by comparison!" he says.

How much time Strong spends in the Level 4 lab depends on what he is doing, but since a lot of his research is carried out on cell cultures and infected cells, he is in the lab most days—including weekends, during an experiment—but usually not for much longer than two or three hours at a time. Occasionally, however, an experiment will require him or other researchers to be in the lab several times during the day and through the night.

A Long Process

The process of entering the Level 4 lab starts long before Strong dons the "space suit," with much of the prep work occurring in the Level 2 area (see sidebar). That work includes culturing—growing—the cells that will be infected with the virus inside the lab and gathering any necessary supplies that have to be taken into the Level 4 lab.

With supplies ready and everyone notified about his upcoming entry into Level 4, Strong is finally ready to go in.

The first step is to "strip down to what you're born with," Strong says. After that, he puts on surgical scrubs before entering through a big set of double doors, only

Infectious Disease Specialists

opened by a large hand crank. Once inside the room, he dons the protective suit.

The suits are constantly checked to ensure they are secure. Each time one is used, the researcher carefully inspects it visually. Once a week, the suits are filled with air and examined to make certain they have not sprung any leaks.

After examining the suit, Strong puts it on and makes sure it is sealed. Outside, every researcher has a "backup buddy," a person with whom a researcher in the lab can stay in constant contact, usually by radio. That way, if a problem occurs, someone outside the lab is immediately aware of it. Researchers tell their backup buddy how long they plan to be in the lab, and what they will be doing inside.

After passing through another set of double doors with a chemical shower between them, Strong enters the Level 4 suites. The chemical shower automatically activates as soon as he passes through, decontaminating the room between the doors that has just been opened to the Level 4 area.

Finally, in Strong's words, "you call out to your radio buddy: 'I am going to Level 4.'"

Inside the Lab

Inside the lab itself, the work that is carried out is not very different from similar work on less-dangerous germs. The deadly viruses themselves, however, are stored in liquid nitrogen, which keeps them frozen and

JAMES STRONG: SCIENCE IN A SPACE SUIT

Each week, the "space suits" are filled with air to make sure they don't have any holes in them. Even a tiny hole could let a virus in and be potentially dangerous for a researcher.

Infectious Disease Specialists

inactive. Their removal from storage is tightly controlled. Researchers must tell others ahead of time that they are removing a virus sample and note the exact quantities being taken out. They also must let others know what the sample of the virus is to be used for and how they plan to dispose of it.

All of that is to ensure nothing potentially infectious is left somewhere where it might pose a risk to researchers or could possibly be carried out of the lab.

The Level 4 "space suits" are easier to move around in than one might think. As Strong says: "Most people find them quite comfortable, unless they just do not like enclosed spaces."

Each researcher tends to wear the same suit every time he or she goes in, although frequent users often share a suit with researchers who only go in once in a while. The researchers wear triple gloves—two thinner inner gloves and a thicker outer one—which cut down on sensation, but this is no different from what a surgeon would wear to perform some types of surgery. Nevertheless, it takes much longer to perform any task in Level 4 than it would in an ordinary Level 2 lab, especially when you figure in the time needed just to get in and out.

"If it was going to take you fifteen minutes on the outside, it would take you more like an hour or an hour-and-a-half on the inside with all the preparation work," Strong says.

JAMES STRONG: SCIENCE IN A SPACE SUIT

Although the researchers wear triple gloves and "space suits" in the Level 4 lab, they are still able to move around freely.

Infectious Disease Specialists

Inconvenient but Peaceful

Despite the inconvenience of getting in and out, Strong enjoys working in the Level 4 lab. "It is quite peaceful. You have the nice white background, a gentle breeze on your face, and a little bit of white noise. And you don't have pagers and cell phones and other things going off in there."

That is important, because even with all the precautions, "You want to stay focused," Strong says. "You are not often being tapped on the shoulder and being asked, 'Excuse me, would you pass the pipettes?' or something like that. You get a heightened sense of both personal space and focus."

There are never very many people working in Level 4 at the same time. Regulations allow for up to ten people between the National Microbiology Laboratory's Level 4 lab and the Canadian Food Inspection Agency's Level 4 lab, housed in the same building. However, two to six is more typical, with six being much less common than two.

Even though everything possible is done to make the Level 4 lab safe to work in, Strong says he never forgets he is working with deadly viruses. "I think it is always in your head." Strong always stays alert to possible risks: "In a Level 2 lab, if you were to knock something off [the work bench], you might end up reaching quickly to grab for it. In Level 4 you are much more cautious about it. You don't make any quick movements."

The biggest risk is puncturing both the suit and your skin. A small hole in the suit is not particularly dangerous, because the air inside it is at a higher pressure than the air in the lab, meaning that lab air cannot get in through a small puncture. And the lab air itself is completely renewed every three minutes by a special ventilation system.

"You occasionally do get a hole in the glove," Strong says, "which means that you have to quickly dunk your hand into some disinfectant and take yourself out of that environment."

Even when the researchers are working with the viruses, he notes, the work is done inside a biosafety hood or cabinet. "Certainly the risk of exposure is very, very low, even with a punctured suit."

Decontamination

When the time comes to leave, all the materials used in the experiment are carefully secured and put away. Then it is time for decontamination.

The researchers dunk their hands in disinfectant to kill any microorganisms that might have somehow managed to attach themselves, then exit into the chemical shower, located between the set of double doors. Still wearing the suit, they take a five-minute shower: two minutes of MicroChem (a disinfectant chemical) and three minutes of water to rinse off the MicroChem, scrubbing at the same time to clean off anything sticky that might be on the suit. Strong says researchers also rinse off their air

Infectious Disease Specialists

hoses to make sure nothing got in when the hoses were hooked up or disconnected.

No more than two people can be in the chemical shower at the same time. Once the shower is over, the researchers go through the second door into the suit-change area. They take off their suits, then peel off their surgical scrubs and take a personal shower at least three minutes long. After that, they put on their regular clothes and exit the lab.

"Did You Wash Your Hands Today?"

Strong enjoys his research in what he calls "a fairly untapped area."

"A lot of [research subjects] that you can apply to other viruses have not been studied [with the Level 4 viruses] because of the nature of the organisms and the nature of the level of containment that you need. So anything you can shed light on is brand new. I think that is probably the best thing about it."

He does not consider himself a daredevil for working in a Level 4 lab. "When I got into it originally I thought, 'Wow, that would be so cool to try to do this stuff in a Level 4 lab and be involved in outbreaks and things like that.' But now," he says, "it is pretty much the same as you would do in a normal Level 2 lab; you just have to have the added time and pain-in-the-butt factor of putting on a suit, chemical showers—that sort of thing."

JAMES STRONG: SCIENCE IN A SPACE SUIT

Every researcher who enters or leaves the Level 4 lab must go through a chemical shower to ensure that no outside elements can interfere with the research, and that no potentially dangerous disease specimens are carried outside the lab.

He admits, though, that when he tells people outside the lab what he does for a living, they are sometimes reluctant to shake his hand.

"People always ask, 'Did you wash your hands today?'" he laughs. "But sometimes if I've gone into Level 4 I am cleaner than anybody, because I have had six personal showers by the time I am done with my day!"

Coral reefs are diverse ecosystems with over a million species of marine life. Unfortunately, they are threatened by a number of factors, including disease.

Chapter 4

LAURIE RICHARDSON

Stalking the Coral Killer

You'd think microbiology would mean you spend most of your time looking at bacteria through a microscope. You wouldn't expect it to lead you to spending days scuba diving. But for Dr. Laurie Richardson, that's exactly where it led—and in a way it led home, since she grew up on and in the water.

Today, Richardson is a professor of biology at Florida International University (FIU) in Miami. Her research is focused on black band disease in coral reefs.

There are 110,900 square miles of coral reefs in the world's oceans. That sounds like a lot, but it is less than one tenth of one percent of the total area of the ocean floor. Despite their small size, however, coral reefs play an important role in the health of the ocean, because they support more than a million species of marine life. They are also important to the humans who live near the oceans. Coral reefs and the organisms that live on and around them provide food for many tropical islanders and also attract tourists.

However, coral reefs are dying from pollution, overfishing, and a variety of diseases—including Richardson's focus, black band disease. In fact, scientists predict that if nothing changes, 90 percent of the world's coral reefs could be threatened by 2030.[1]

A Land-Locked Education

Despite having grown up near the water, Richardson started college just about as far away from the ocean as possible—in Boulder, Colorado. She majored in fine arts, chemistry, and environmental biology, then went on to get her PhD in microbiology.

Her focus in her PhD research was "microbial mats," communities of microbes that live in the sulfur-rich water that flows out of hot springs. From there she went to Wisconsin where she worked on a NASA research project with scientists who were using data from satellites to study aquatic ecosystems. They needed someone like Richardson who was knowledgeable about bacteria that are photosynthetic—bacteria that, like plants, can make their own food when exposed to sunlight.

She eventually arrived in Florida with a NASA-funded grant to work on algal pigments (the compounds

LAURIE RICHARDSON: STALKING THE CORAL KILLER

Dr. Laurie Richardson is a microbiologist and biology professor who studies black band disease in coral.

> **Infectious Disease Specialists**

that give algae their color) and remote sensing—she did not know that her work in hot springs and bacteria would both come into play.

One day, just for fun, she went scuba diving on a coral reef, and somebody asked her what she thought about the algae killing the corals. "They showed me black band disease on the reef," Richardson explains. "I took one look at it and could see immediately that it was exactly like the kind of microbial communities that are found in hot spring outflows. And then I looked in the literature, and nobody had done anything at all with these communities. And that was how my whole research started."[2]

That kind of "aha!" moment, that sudden grasp of a previously unknown connection, is what makes science exciting, Richardson says. "These days they call that interdisciplinary science. Somebody from another discipline [field of science] comes and looks at a problem and says, 'Hey! That's obvious! Look at what is going on!'"

Working Underwater

Most of Richardson's day-to-day time is spent teaching, writing papers and proposals, or working in her laboratory, but she also spends a good deal of time out in the ocean with graduate students, undergraduate students, and research collaborators. Together they collect samples and monitor the progress of disease on the reef. Most of that work takes place during "disease

LAURIE RICHARDSON: STALKING THE CORAL KILLER

A recreational scuba diving outing, like the one shown here, prompted Richardson's research into the algae in coral reefs.

> **Infectious Disease Specialists**

season," which is summertime in the Florida Keys and off the islands of the Bahamas.

Richardson assembles a team for each "mission," during which they dive every day for ten days—she refers to that time as the "intense field work." After that, they return to the lab and work with samples they have collected.

On a typical mission day, the team prepares all of their pieces of equipment: sterile sampling syringes, sterile vials for samples, plastic and mesh bags, diving equipment, underwater slates, and coolers, to name a few. The research boat leaves the dock at about eight in the morning. The team also comes prepared to work safely: "Once we are on the reef we always have a very specific field plan of who is diving with who, and what samples we are going to get."

Coral samples are taken with numbered, sterilized syringes. "When you are underwater, you just reach your hand into your bag and grab one syringe by random, take your sample, and then record very carefully on your slate the number on the syringe and what that sample is, and a description of the diseased coral."

The day's work isn't done when they return to shore. From processing samples to transcribing all of the data collected that day into a computer file or field notebook, there are sometimes several hours of work before a day is truly complete. It makes for a long, hard day, Richardson says. "But it's fun, too!"

At least, most of the time.

LAURIE RICHARDSON: STALKING THE CORAL KILLER

Richardson and her team do their fieldwork underwater—taking samples, measurements, and descriptions of coral. They use their findings to monitor disease on the coral.

The Hazards of Diving

One risk of diving is decompression sickness, also known as "the bends." While a diver is underwater his or her body is compressed by the weight of the water above. Gases can dissolve in the bloodstream under pressure. When the diver surfaces, the gases expand, forming bubbles in the bloodstream that can cause extreme pain. They can even be life-threatening.

Richardson recalled one mission where she got the bends while exploring a reef along what they call a "transect line"—this is simply a straight line marked across an area where scientists are taking samples. The

Infectious Disease Specialists

A diver breathes oxygen after staying deep underwater for too long.

researchers follow the line and take samples at regular intervals.

"It took an hour," Richardson explains, "going down along this transect and counting the number of diseased corals and then coming back, very slow and very gradual."

Over the next two dives they did a disease survey, counting corals and taking note of which species were present and which were diseased. To do that, one diver swam in circles with a line tethered to a fixed point at the circle's center. While that diver counted diseased and healthy corals, the second diver made sure the line didn't get caught on anything.

Keeping an eye on that line was Richardson's job. This meant she wasn't doing much actual swimming while being in the freezing cold water. On her last dive (of only eight feet) Richardson was performing some heavy work with an underwater drill, trying to loosen some black band–infected coral for sampling. Going from the calm of monitoring a line to using a heavy drill in the freezing water, Richardson ended up getting decompression sickness—the bends.

To treat the bends, Richardson says, "They put you in a pressurized chamber and increase the pressure in there comparable to the depth of sixty feet of water. You are breathing pure oxygen."

While she was well within the safety guidelines to prevent decompression sickness, it is "just something that can happen when you are out there working and

Infectious Disease Specialists

you dive hundreds and thousands of times," Richardson says.

Caught in a Surge

Something even scarier happened on another dive, when Richardson's research team was working in the Bahamas near Bemini, off a fairly large, anchored research boat.

A strong surge—the term for a powerful underwater current—came up, pulling sediment from the ocean floor, which ruined the team's visibility. Richardson and the two graduate students with her had to grab metal bars

A decompression chamber is used to treat decompression sickness, also known as the bends.

planted in the ocean floor and pull themselves blindly in the direction where they thought the anchor was.

"Fortunately we found the anchor, because if we had got caught in that current and got away from the boat we would have been off in the Gulf Stream [current] and who knows where...," Richardson said.

The coral itself poses some risk to divers as well. Corals are living animals, with an extremely thin layer of living tissue (often less than a millimeter—one twenty-fifth of an inch—thick) over a rocklike skeleton of calcium carbonate. "If you grab onto them or get knocked into them or if your buoyancy control is bad and you crash into them . . . and break that tissue then that is really sharp rock. You're going to get cut," Richardson warns.

"There are a lot of bacteria that live in association with the surface of the coral. You can get a really nasty infection." But, she says, "We do our best not to do that." And fortunately, it has never happened to her.

Richardson is quick to add that "there are a lot of nice things that happen down there, too." She recalls a time when she was doing a five-day study of the progression of black band disease that required her to be underwater for four or five hours a day. Near the reef she was studying lived some grouper fish that would peek around the corners of the coral and watch her. Some of them even followed her around. "It was amazing," she says. "To this day I won't eat grouper because of that experience."

Infectious Disease Specialists

Solving a Puzzle

Richardson began her research on coral diseases around 1990. After more than fifteen years, she says she is beginning to put together the pieces of the complex puzzle that makes up black band disease. It is complicated because it is a poly-microbial disease, which means it is caused by a whole bunch of different microbes working together.

"We haven't figured it out yet, but it has gotten to the point where it is like a jigsaw puzzle that is maybe seven-

Richardson and her colleagues are starting to put together the pieces of the black band disease puzzle. They have discovered that the mysterious black bands are caused by bacteria releasing gas that is toxic to coral—probably due in part to global warming.

eighths of the way filled in. Anything we figure out now is one more piece of the puzzle, so that is really exciting."

What they have figured out so far is that as the disease-causing community of bacteria (dominated by blue-green algae) first grows, it quickly consumes the available oxygen. That opens the door for another group of bacteria, present in the ocean all the time, that thrive in an oxygen-free environment. Instead of oxygen, these bacteria use a compound called sulfate, which is dissolved in seawater, as a source of energy. They produce sulfide gas as a waste product.

"It turns out that sulfide gas is toxic to coral, and that starts killing the coral tissue. The dying coral tissue is then a source of nutrients and organic carbon for more bacteria. We also found out that the blue-green algae produce another toxin."

Unfortunately, she says, the main problem seems to be global warming. Global warming upsets the normal balance between corals and their environment.

"We work on corals in tropical and subtropical reefs, and so they live in warm water, but when the water gets too warm they become stressed out. It's like us—if we are too cold our immune system doesn't really work that well." Corals don't really have an immune system, she says, but the problem is still similar.

Although the warmer water stresses the corals, microorganisms love it. When water temperatures go up, Richardson says, the growth of bacteria and blue-green algae "takes off like a rocket."

Infectious Disease Specialists

"In the meantime the corals they are living on become stressed and cannot defend themselves against infections, and what you get is disease."

Biologists may not be able to do anything about global warming, Richardson says, "but at least we can have some evidence that says this is a big part of the problem and people should really do something serious about global warming."

The work continues to be rewarding, Richardson says, for a couple of reasons. "We really do feel that we are figuring out what is going on with coral diseases."

They have new tools at their disposal, too, as technology advances. "We are now using metagenomics and metabolomics as well as fieldwork and classical microbiology," she says.

Metagenomics is the study of genetic material that is taken from environmental samples like those Richardson retrieves from the coral reefs. Integrating the genomic information with the information gathered in the field about how the microbes function in their communities can shed light on the structure of those communities.[3] Metabolomics is the study of the unique chemical fingerprints that cellular processes leave behind.[4]

Richardson's research into how microbes function in communities may also shed light on human diseases—in fact, she's received funding from the National Institutes of Health (NIH). Many human diseases are also caused by a community of bacteria rather than a single type of germ, but it is difficult to study those kinds of communities of bacteria in humans.

"You can't have humans being your lab rats," Richardson explains. However, she can take samples of the reef and try to better understand how many different microorganisms work together to cause disease.

Her work is also, Richardson notes, a wonderful teaching model. "I'm a biology professor, and my students are learning all about ecology [how organisms relate to their environment and other organisms] and physiology [how living organisms work] and microbiology and molecular genetics while they're out there in this incredible environment working on the reef."

What Does It Take to Be a Microbiologist?

For students who want to pursue a similar career, and maybe work in a similarly incredible environment, Richardson's advice is simple: "I always tell students the same thing: keep your grades up . . . keep your options open. Then when the time comes for you to make that decision and really pursue that career, you can be accepted into any program that you want to do."

This kind of work is very competitive, Richardson warns. "If you have not kept your grades up, and you go there and you apply . . . You'll get turned away right at the door."

And then, of course, you have to continue to keep your grades up all through college and graduate school,

Infectious Disease Specialists

Richardson hopes that her research in the coral reefs will help raise awareness of the effects of global warming.

then try to get into a lab with somebody who is doing the kind of work you want to do.

Achieving that puts you in a position to take advantage of opportunities as they come along—just as Richardson did when she started working in remote sensing with NASA and ended up recognizing a microbial mat on a diseased reef in Florida during a dive just for fun.

How much the job pays depends on who is paying. If you are teaching at a university, you are paid a nine-month salary, and then are free to find research grants or do summer teaching over the remaining months. "These days starting salaries for assistant professors in Biology (tenure track) are $75,000 at FIU. The highest paid full professors are about $120,000. But that is going to depend on the university. For a small university, or colleges, it is usually less than that."

"Like Being a Kid All Your Life"

Money is important, but it is not the most important thing, Richardson says. "It is really fun to be a scientist and make discoveries and figure out problems and make a story and piece together . . . what is going on with really complex interactions between species. That is really satisfying and rewarding." As a friend of Richardson's likes to say, "Being a scientist is like being a kid all your life." A kid, in Richardson's case, who gets to spend her summers diving on coral reefs.

A young man protects himself with a face mask during an avian flu outbreak in Asia. Scientist Jonathan Runstadler is studying the bird population of Alaska to find out how avian flu is spread.

Chapter 5

JONATHAN RUNSTADLER

The Biology of Bird Flu

Alaska is home to more than 470 species of birds. Some of the birds stay in Alaska year-round, but most—millions every year—migrate to Canada, Central America, South America, Asia, or the lower forty-eight United States, returning to Alaska each spring to breed. They include waterfowl (such as geese and ducks) shorebirds (curlews and sandpipers), raptors (hawks and eagles), and land birds (warblers, sparrows, and crows).[1]

Some of these birds spend the winter in South America, Central America, or southern North America. But some of them spend the winter in Southeast Asia, home to a strain of avian influenza (bird flu) called H5N1, which is so virulent it kills 100 percent of some poultry species within forty-eight hours.

Infectious Disease Specialists

H5N1 can also infect humans. The first known infection of a human occurred in 1997 during a poultry outbreak in Hong Kong. The virus re-emerged in 2003 and 2004, and since then has spread from Asia to Europe and Africa, becoming entrenched in the poultry population in some countries, resulting in millions of infections.[2] As of February 2015, there had also been 694 human cases worldwide, resulting in 402 deaths.[3]

Many scientists fear this virus (or one of several other avian influenza virus types, such as H7N9, which has also infected a few people),[4] may eventually become a form of the flu that could kill millions of people worldwide in a global pandemic, an epidemic that spreads across a particularly large area.

In January 2015, staff check the grounds around a goose farm in Taiwan to prevent the spread of bird flu. Other birds in the area tested positive for the H5 strain of the flu.

It has happened before. An influenza pandemic in 1918 killed an estimated fifty million people, many of them healthy young adults. That set it apart from more common strains of influenza. Influenza kills thousands every year, but normally only those who are very elderly, very young, or already in a weakened condition due to other health problems.

Recently, scientists identified the virus that caused the 1918 pandemic as a strain of avian influenza. It jumped directly from birds to humans, and mutated, or changed, so it could be easily passed from person to person.

Although the H5N1 virus has not yet shown up in North America, viruses related to it have. And if H5N1 does make it to North America, a prime place for it to make its first appearance, because of the number of migratory birds that breed there, is Alaska.

And that's why Dr. Jonathan Runstadler, assistant professor of biological engineering and comparative medicine in the Biological Engineering Department at the Massachusetts Institute of Technology, spends a lot of time in the summer swabbing the bottoms of Alaskan birds.

Learning How Influenza Circulates in Birds

The goal of Runstadler's efforts is to learn more about how avian influenza viruses—of which there are more than 140 different types—circulate in Alaska's birds, while also keeping an eye out for H5N1.

Infectious Disease Specialists

The project began in 2005. Many people besides Runstadler are involved. They take a swab of each bird's cloaca (the opening in a bird's rear end through which both urine and feces are expelled) and in some cases also obtain a swab from the bird's trachea, the breathing tube that carries air from the beak to the lungs. Sometimes they also collect samples of blood and feathers in order to examine the bird's genetic makeup.

Runstadler and his team are not capturing birds by themselves. Instead, they take advantage of some of the many other bird studies going on in Alaska at any given time.

"In Alaska, there is a lot of interest in bird work," Runstadler says. "A lot of people [go] up there to work on bird populations that breed and nest there and [raise] their young. What we have done is connect with those people and go out with them on field projects where they are getting their hands on birds."[5]

Runstadler says there are many projects to choose from. For several seasons he worked with a researcher named Jim Sedinger, who was studying Brant geese in the Yukon flats. Sedinger's team waited until the geese were molting (replacing old feathers with new ones) and were mostly unable to fly. Then they herded the geese down long, thin bits of land, bordered on either side by streams entering the Bering Sea, into temporary pens. "There can be anywhere from a hundred to a thousand geese at any one of these herdings," Runstadler says.

JONATHAN RUNSTADLER: THE BIOLOGY OF BIRD FLU

Jonathan Runstadler spends much of his time in the field herding and swabbing birds. He tests the swab samples he collects for viruses—including avian flu.

Infectious Disease Specialists

Sedinger's team members collected data on the birds' ages and molt status, and put metal bands on their legs so individual birds could be identified if they were captured another time. Runstadler and his colleagues collected their samples at the same time.

Another major site for Runstadler's team's work was the Alaskan interior, not far from Fairbanks. There, with the Alaskan Department of Fish and Game, they banded and captured birds, taking samples along the way.

A third major sampling site was within the city of Fairbanks itself, where the now-closed Alaska Bird Observatory did a lot of sampling of songbirds, which they captured using mist nets. (A mist net is a fine-meshed net, similar to a volleyball net, that is invisible to the birds as they fly through the trees.)

In 2015 Runstadler's team is working on a project examining the virus in gull populations in South Central Alaska around the city of Cordova.

> "Recently, we've seen viruses related to H5N1 show up in North America, and so have restarted some additional sampling in Alaska to see if those strains are circulating more widely than we thought. We've also started other projects, particularly in New England, where we have begun a new, but related, project to examine how influenza virus is affecting the growing marine mammal populations in New England. I spent several days this past January restraining seal pups for sampling in frigid weather on Cape Cod. It was cold, hard work, but worth it to work on the incredible animals and even more so to work with a great and diverse group of people from federal agencies (like

JONATHAN RUNSTADLER: THE BIOLOGY OF BIRD FLU

> ## ❗ Camping and Flying
>
> **Working in the field** in Alaska means a lot of camping, Runstadler says, although some of the work done near Fairbanks can be completed on day trips. Larger bird samplings, especially waterfowl samplings, involve weeklong or even two-week-long trips. For these samplings, Runstadler and his fellow researchers go out to field camps. "Sometimes those are pretty nice field camps. The Minto Flats area, where we do a lot of duck sampling, has a cabin that has a generator, and so people cook and so forth. Sometimes it's just tents and a regular camp site."
>
> How do they get there? There is really only one way.
>
> "In Alaska," Runstadler says, "you get everywhere by flying." Getting to the bigger sampling sites usually involves a trip in a floatplane. "That's a lot of fun!"

National Oceanic and Atmospheric Administration, Fish and Wildlife Service, and National Parks) as well as volunteers from other research groups and individuals (New England Aquarium, Mystic Aquarium, Stranding network groups, etc.). We camped in an old lighthouse at the Monomoy Refuge in Chatham, huddled around propane heaters, but glad to be there."

Foraging for Feces

In Alaska, in addition to collecting samples directly from birds, Runstadler's team samples the birds' environments.

Infectious Disease Specialists

Runstadler and a colleague swab a bird's cloaca, the opening from which wastes are expelled.

"It's a big question mark as to what happens when the bird deposits the virus in the environment," Runstadler says.

It is thought that the virus stays in the bird population because infected birds leave waste in the environment. Other birds then pick up the virus by drinking contaminated water or mucking around in contaminated mud.

Runstadler's team samples mud and water in the summer and ice and frozen mud in the winter. They drill out ice cores and take mud samples from beneath the ice at the edges of frozen ponds, then look at those samples

JONATHAN RUNSTADLER: THE BIOLOGY OF BIRD FLU

"both to detect virus and then see if we can grow virus from those samples."

The goal is to determine if environmental factors have an impact on the persistence of the virus and if the viruses can survive the winter and infect birds arriving in Alaska the following spring.

An Interest in Animals

Runstadler grew up with a strong interest in animals and the environment. When he enrolled at Stanford University in California, it was natural for him to study biology.

Scientists acquire samples from the birds' environments, like lakes, ponds, and marshes, in order to fully understand how the virus is transmitted.

Infectious Disease Specialists

After he graduated, he worked for two different companies for a couple of years. One grew scallops in the Cape Cod area. The other was trying to develop an ecology-based method of processing wastewater (the water that goes down the drains in your house).

His experience with those companies boosted his interest in research, so he decided to go to graduate school. He intended to get a doctorate in molecular evolution, the study of the changes in DNA that drive evolution. However, just as he arrived at the University of New Hampshire in the early 1990s, the university launched a new program combining laboratory-based molecular science with environmental or ecology-based projects. That ended up being what he focused on.

That, in turn, got him interested in veterinary medicine. Runstadler ended up getting a dual PhD and doctor of veterinary medicine degree from the University of California at Davis. After about ten years in Davis, he moved to Fairbanks, where he became assistant professor of biology and wildlife at the University of Alaska Fairbanks Institute of Arctic Biology.

"One of the reasons why I decided to accept the position in Fairbanks is Fairbanks has a strong history in studies in ecology, environmental science, and wildlife biology," Runstadler said. The university also had several research projects underway in which Runstadler thought molecular lab-based science could be used to answer questions that came up during work in the field. One of those was the study of avian influenza. Runstadler

JONATHAN RUNSTADLER: THE BIOLOGY OF BIRD FLU

thought it would be interesting to learn more about avian influenza and how it could spread around the world. He also thought it would be interesting to learn how species that carry the disease are themselves affected by it.

"All of these different duck species seem to inhabit similar ecologies [habitats], have similar lifestyles, do similar things, and yet when we go out and sample them and look for influenza, we get different types of viruses," Runstadler says. One aim of his research is to understand why some species are more likely to be infected by the

A young boy walks by a poultry market in China. Scientists like Runstadler hope that their research will uncover the chain of events that leads avian flu to spread from wild birds to domestic birds—and sometimes to humans.

Infectious Disease Specialists

virus, and therefore more likely to be carrying it from place to place.

Runstadler says his team is working with other biologists more and more to determine what effect the viruses have on birds in the wild. "In some of the areas that we study, up to 20 percent of birds are infected with influenza virus."

The researchers are also trying to find out how this reservoir of virus in wild birds relates to the occasional outbreak of influenza in domestic birds such as chickens—and vice versa. "Is there a movement back and forth? Who is to blame?"

In the fall of 2011, Runstadler moved his laboratory to the Massachusetts Institute of Technology (MIT). His goal, in addition to being closer to family, was to be able to conduct more experimental work exploring how bird flu behaves in nature. Specifically, he wanted to look at how the virus grows and changes in different hosts, while also exploring how its genetic makeup interacts with the environment.

As well, he adds, "MIT is a great place to be with lots of interaction with people doing innovative and creative work in biology, engineering, and many other fields related to our work. It helps everyone stay interested and creative and attracts great students!"

Meet Your Local Scientists

Runstadler urges young people who are interested in pursuing a career in science to get acquainted with

JONATHAN RUNSTADLER: THE BIOLOGY OF BIRD FLU

It All Started with Weasels

Runstadler grew up in Hanover, New Hampshire, home to Dartmouth College and the Montshire Museum of Science, a hands-on science museum for kids. Runstadler took his first steps along the road to being a scientist in the fifth grade, when he did a school project on weasels. For that science project, students had to choose an animal and do a lot of research and writing about it.

"I chose the weasel—for what reason I can't exactly remember—and it so happened that the science education person who was in charge of the museum at the time was having an exhibit on weasels. I remember calling up and asking if I could meet with him and going over and talking with him about weasels.

"That's one of the things that I remember that influenced me, talking to somebody who was a scientist and who was interested in education. It was not just a book that I picked up and read about weasels. It was somebody that I talked to, and it was an exhibit that showed live weasels."

He even arranged to have a demonstration in his classroom of how the weasels were fed, but the school wouldn't allow it, fearing how kids (and likely their parents) might react to a weasel eating live mice in the classroom. Runstadler remembers it all with humor: "My science project was censored!"

Infectious Disease Specialists

scientists in their community. "Usually those people are happy to help," he says.

By way of example, Runstadler points out that in the Fairbanks area there are people at the university whose job it is to spread around their interest and knowledge. Many high school students have worked with the faculty at the university on research projects, sometimes for several years before they go to college. Sometimes they continue working on projects even after they have gone to college.

"I think the best thing to do is contact people in the community who are doing this work or work that's related to it," Runstadler says. Young people who get involved in research projects like his usually discover they love it, he adds.

"There are a lot of things you can do as a kid your parents can help you with," he continues. "There are a lot of resources out there now for doing projects around your house or doing projects you find out about in the community that need volunteers. Maybe they need somebody to count birds during migration season—that can sometimes be done with just counting birds that come to your bird feeder during a certain time of year.

"There are more and more projects like that that are looking for a pool of volunteers to gather information. That is sometimes a lead-in to going further with projects or contacting other people."

Runstadler admits that spending part of your summer catching birds and taking swabs from their rear ends

JONATHAN RUNSTADLER: THE BIOLOGY OF BIRD FLU

Bird counting is a simple way to get involved in the scientific community. Many groups conduct counts during migration season in order to track various bird species.

sounds strange. "I take a lot of grief for being somebody who looks at the bottom end of birds. But there are a lot of aspects of it that are enjoyable." That includes the fieldwork, he says, but also learning about the birds, "what they do, and what's special about them."

Runstadler says he has never had a scary moment, whether through direct contact with the birds or during his air travels throughout Alaska. But he does admit it is a bit scary thinking about the potential of picking up an infection from all the birds he handles.

Runstadler says that most experts in the field of influenza believe that at some point there will be a pandemic or very large outbreak that affects human populations.

> Some have been convinced that it is going to happen with this H5N1 virus—some are convinced that it might be that one, but it might well be another one that we don't have our eye on as closely. The fact that there are viruses out there . . . that can potentially kill you is something that gives you second thoughts when you're out sampling those birds. But that's really some of the motivation of it. Some of the work we do might lead to an understanding of these viruses that makes them less scary and dangerous on the whole.

That would be good news for all of us, even those of us who have never seen a bird's bottom.

Chapter 6

LISA FERNANDO

An Outbreak of Marburg

"You've got to be kidding me!" Lisa Fernando had just been told she would be flying to the African nation of Angola within a week.[1] It was 2005 and she was going to help battle an outbreak of Marburg hemorrhagic fever. Hemorrhagic fevers are particularly nasty diseases whose symptoms typically include a high fever and, worst of all, internal bleeding: Victims can bleed to death inside their own skins.

Fernando had been working at the Canadian Science Centre for Human and Animal Health in Winnipeg, Manitoba, for two and a half years. She had started there shortly after she received her master's degree in medical microbiology—the study of microscopic bacteria and viruses that cause disease.

Infectious Disease Specialists

The Canadian Science Centre for Human and Animal Health is a joint facility, home to both the Public Health Agency of Canada's National Microbiology Laboratory and the Canadian Food Inspection Agency's National Centre for Foreign Animal Disease. It is also home to the country's only Level 4 laboratory. A Level 4 laboratory, like the ones described in Chapter 3, is one that can meet the strict safety standards for working with some of the world's most dangerous disease-causing agents, such as the Marburg virus.

Marburg is closely related to the Ebola virus, one of the best-known disease-causing agents that scientists study in Level 4 labs. But until the outbreak in Angola,

Lisa Fernando traveled to Angola, Africa, to help during an outbreak of Marburg hemorrhagic fever.

86

confirmed by the World Health Organization (WHO) in March 2005, nobody realized that Marburg could be just as deadly as Ebola.

There is no cure for Marburg hemorrhagic fever, just as there is no cure for Ebola. A person can easily become infected if he or she is in contact with bodily fluids, such as blood, from an infected person. At the time Fernando got the call to go to Angola, nine out of every ten people infected during the outbreak had died.

Surprise and a Bit of Fear

Even though the call to go to Angola had surprised her, Fernando was no stranger to working with deadly viruses. She had been training to do just that for her two and a half years at the Winnipeg lab. "Working with these viruses every day, I really had developed a comfort level," she said. "I felt well-prepared."

Still, when Dr. Heinz Feldmann, chief of special pathogens at the Public Health Agency of Canada—and Fernando's supervisor—told her she was going to Angola, her surprise was tinged with just a bit of fear. It would be her first overseas mission.

She battled the fear with logic, reminding herself, "We're not visiting the people in the field, and for the samples that we're handling, we're following all the same safety requirements as we do in Winnipeg." The only difference, she said, was that in the field they would not have "the fancy Level 4 lab."

Infectious Disease Specialists

The Marburg virus as it is seen under a microscope. Marburg is a rare and deadly hemorraghic fever that is in the same family as Ebola.

88

LISA FERNANDO: AN OUTBREAK OF MARBURG

Fernando knew she had been well trained, and she had a tremendous amount of trust in Feldmann. "He would never bring us into an area where he was worried about our safety or well-being," said Fernando, "I just had to trust in his experience."

Feldmann knew exactly what the team would be getting into, because he was already in Angola. He had gone there as part of the first team Canada sent, along with a mobile laboratory containing the equipment needed to diagnose Marburg. After three weeks in Angola, Feldmann found that the number of cases was increasing and the demand for the lab remained high. That was when he called for Fernando and medical officer Jim Strong to relieve him and his lab assistant.

"I didn't quite totally believe it until I was actually on the plane with Jim," Fernando said. In the week before they left for Angola, there had been too much planning and too many questions to concentrate on the reality of the situation. And, Fernando remembered, "With us being so far away, it was hard to really know what the situation was."

Primitive Conditions

The outbreak began in the northern Angolan city of Uige (pronounced WEEJ). Getting there was not easy. The scientists had to fly into Luanda, the capital of Angola, and then transfer to a tiny four-seat plane for an additional hour-long flight. "I remember the first flight out," Fernando said. "The pilot leaned over, pulled the

Infectious Disease Specialists

door shut, and said, 'Just don't lean on it.' And I thought, 'This is the last flight I will ever take.' But at least it was adventurous!"

Conditions were primitive in Uige. The city and the surrounding countryside were badly affected by the civil war that had gripped Angola until just a couple of years before the outbreak. Fernando remembers the city being war-torn, with blown-out windows, gunshot holes, and dusty, deserted streets.

She and Strong were put up in a hotel . . . of sorts. They had to share one room, which they called the "honeymoon suite" because, unlike the other rooms, it had an attached bathroom. However, the bathroom did not have running water. "The shower was a bucket

WHO specialists visit Uige, Angola, after the Marburg outbreak.

shower," Fernando said. "You had a big tub of water which they would cart in every second day at least, and then you would just bucket-shower that way." They used bottled water to brush their teeth. There was an air-conditioning unit, but no electricity to run it. The food was not always of the highest quality, either. Almost everyone on the expedition had diarrhea at some point.

A Complete Lab in Rubber Bins

The words "mobile laboratory" might make you imagine a gleaming air-conditioned semitrailer. The mobile lab Fernando and Strong worked in, however, was nothing of the sort. It had "no air-conditioning, no running water," Fernando said. Everything in it had been transported to Angola in six to eight rubber bins. The bins had simply been put aboard airplanes as checked luggage. Once the lab was delivered on-site, it could be up and operating within two hours.

The mobile lab contained various test kits; a generator; a laptop computer designed to withstand humidity, dust, and heat; and a satellite phone. It also contained personal protection equipment to ensure the scientists did not infect themselves as they worked with samples from patients.

Using the lab, workers could determine who was infected and who was not. They did not want uninfected people to come into contact with infected people and catch the disease. They hoped to bring the outbreak

Infectious Disease Specialists

A lab technician works in a mobile lab similar to the one used by Fernando in her work with the Marburg outbreak.

under control by keeping the infected people away from the uninfected people.

The most important piece of equipment in the lab was a device called a real-time polymerase chain reaction (RT-PCR) unit. The RT-PCR could make many copies of the incredibly tiny bits of genetic material found inside viruses. It is hard to identify a virus if there is not enough of its genetic material to work with. Once there were enough copies, a virus could be identified.

Fernando and the others would receive samples—typically blood samples or swab samples—from people who might be infected with Marburg. They would

LISA FERNANDO: AN OUTBREAK OF MARBURG

examine those samples using RT-PCR to look for the presence of the Marburg virus.

Playing It Safe

The lab was set up in a room at the Uige Provincial Hospital, where the outbreak was first identified. At the time of the outbreak, that hospital and its four doctors were the only healthcare available for the 1.5 million people in the region. Unfortunately, some of the earliest victims of outbreaks of diseases like Marburg and Ebola are often the medical staff at the hospitals where the first patients are taken. The Angola outbreak was no exception. Among the first to die were two doctors and sixteen nurses.

Fernando says that by the time they got there, the doctors running the isolation ward would not even attempt to treat a patient until they had a diagnosis from the lab—because they feared being infected with the disease themselves. That made the Canadians' work doubly important. Fernando says that malaria is a huge problem in the region, and many of the children being brought to the hospital with symptoms similar to Marburg actually had malaria. Malaria can be treated, but the doctors refused to help the children until they were certain they did not have Marburg.

Fernando and Strong were not working directly with patients, but they still had to take precautions because they were dealing with samples that might contain the

Infectious Disease Specialists

Workers at the hospital in Uige, shown here, had to take extreme caution in working with Marburg patients. They relied on scientists like Fernando to make a diagnosis before treatment.

Marburg virus. The lab tests themselves were run on killed virus—virus that could no longer cause disease.

While they were working with potentially live virus, Fernando and Strong wore something similar to the Level 4 "space suit" (described in more detail in chapter 3) they wore in the lab in Canada. The suit had its own battery-operated breathing supply, drawing in air through a High Efficiency Particulate Air (HEPA) filter—a filter so fine even viruses cannot get through it. The suit also had rubber boots, taped at the top, and three pairs of gloves. "It's like wearing this big snowsuit and it gets very, very hot in there," Fernando says. "At times we were in that suit for an hour or two."

Glad to Be Home

After three weeks in the field, Fernando returned home for a month. Then she went back to Angola for another three weeks, because WHO wanted the lab to remain in Angola for three weeks after the last lab-confirmed case.

"We came home . . . the day before Canada Day [July 1], and that was the best Canada Day ever. I remember thinking, 'Flushing toilets! Right on!' I had never been so grateful for running water and electricity!"

So far, Fernando has not been called for another outbreak. But she is ready to go if asked. "If there is the need, absolutely. I think that it is a great humanitarian effort."

Fernando's research in Winnipeg was focused on developing a vaccine for both Marburg and Ebola.

Infectious Disease Specialists

She says that going to Angola really helped her to put her research into perspective. Seeing the effects of the disease in person reinforced for her the importance of her work in Canada.

In the years since, Fernando has been promoted to operations manager of the Level 4 lab in Winnipeg. That makes her responsible for the daily operation of the lab, which includes training, writing new protocols, working with various departments that support the lab, and managing staff.

"I Fell in Love With Bacteria"

When she was growing up, working with deadly viruses was certainly not what Fernando thought she would end up doing as a career. "I had no idea what a Level 4 virus was," she says. Instead, the job just "fell into her lap," when Heinz Feldmann offered her a job as a biologist with the special pathogens group at the Canadian Science Centre for Human and Animal Health shortly after she completed working on her master's degree with him.

But if working with Level 4 viruses was not something she always thought she wanted to do, working in a research lab certainly was. Fernando says she became interested in biology and chemistry in high school and knew early on that she would study science in college.

"My second year I took a [microbiology] course, and I fell in love with bacteria. Then when I finished my degree I knew that I wanted to do research, so doing a master's was the first step in that direction."

She says that it was the best decision she ever made, because it helped her understand exactly what research involved. It also proved to her that she did not want to go on to obtain her PhD. She was not interested in spending time writing grants and papers; instead, she wanted to focus all of her energies on labwork.

Even though she enjoys it, "Research is hard," Fernando says. "We often say in the lab it's 90 percent failure, 10 percent success."

Fernando says she laughs whenever she watches the 1995 movie *Outbreak*, perhaps the best-known fictional version of the kind of work she does. "I love the way they find a cure in 24 hours, and the scientists fall in love. Really, we don't lead glamorous lives like that. Research is hard: it's mostly failure. You get maybe one day of success out of the whole year. You have to be the type of person who can put up with that frustration and be very patient."

"None of Us Are in This for the Glory"

Fernando says the question she was most often asked by media in Canada at the time of the outbreak was, "Do you consider yourself a hero?"

She found it hard to believe anyone would even ask her that question. "Everyone I know in this business, the colleagues of mine that went to Angola, none of us are in this for the glory or the money, because there isn't a lot of money in science," Fernando says. "We're not in this for the front-page news, not at all. We're just here to do our job."

"Take All Your Science Courses"

Lisa Fernando's advice to young people interested in a career like hers is simple and straightforward: "Take all your science courses." Even though she didn't plan on pursuing physics, she says, she still took physics courses.

"Ask lots of questions, and find out about research opportunities," Fernando advises. "During my undergrad degree at the University of Winnipeg, I pursued the honors program which required you to complete a research project and write a thesis. The project I chose was not necessarily in my interest area; we were studying algae!"

Even unrelated research can prove to be a valuable experience: "Although it was completely irrelevant to what I'm doing now, just the process of doing research, understanding that things do not always work out, and realizing the type of traits you need as a researcher—that experience was very helpful." As a result, she suggests anyone interested in becoming a research scientist try to pursue some type of research at college, "whether it be a summer job or a thesis course."

Now that she's operations manager for the Level 4 lab, she's found that her experience with public speaking has been an asset, so she adds one more bit of advice: "If you are willing and able to speak publicly, I think that will help move your career forward!"

Chapter 7

JONATHAN EPSTEIN

Seeking the Source of SARS

Trying to figure out the source of a new disease involves detective work, puzzle-solving…and sometimes a bit of Indiana Jones derring-do, like, say, teetering atop a twenty-foot-tall rocky spire in a cavern in China, trying to string a net to capture bats that may be carrying a deadly disease. Just ask Dr. Jonathan Epstein.

Epstein is a veterinarian epidemiologist with EcoHealth Alliance. In 2004 he led the first expedition into China to try to determine if bats might be the source of the virus that caused the deadly new illness known as Sudden Acute Respiratory Syndrome (SARS). Just two years before, SARS had sickened thousands and killed hundreds around the world.

Infectious Disease Specialists

A New Illness Emerges

The SARS outbreak began on November 16, 2002, when the first case of an unusual form of pneumonia was reported in Guangdong province in southern China. What made it unusual was that it was not caused by any of the usual germs that cause pneumonia. That meant that it also did not respond to the usual treatments.

As more cases of the strange illness began to crop up, the Chinese authorities tried to identify it—without success. But the world at large remained mostly unaware of the disease until, on February 28, 2003, the Vietnam French Hospital of Hanoi contacted the local office of the World Health Organization (WHO). The hospital wanted a doctor from WHO to come take a look at a patient with an unusual influenza-like illness.

Dr. Carlo Urbani responded to the call. He quickly realized that the hospital had a case of something unknown, dangerous—and worst of all, highly contagious. Before long, health workers in the hospital were also falling ill.

Urbani called the disease Sudden Acute Respiratory Syndrome.[1] By mid-March another outbreak of SARS had been reported in Hong Kong, and a patient in Toronto had died from the disease. WHO issued a global alert. There were fears of a global pandemic as SARS cropped up in more than two dozen countries in North America, South America, Europe, and Asia.

In the end, heroic efforts to identify and isolate those who had been exposed to the virus paid off. Within a

JONATHAN EPSTEIN: SEEKING THE SOURCE OF SARS

People in Hong Kong wear masks to protect against the SARS virus in 2003.

few months, no more SARS cases were being reported anywhere. But over the course of the outbreak, 8,098 people had become ill, and 774 had died.[2]

Among those was Carlo Urbani. He contracted the disease at the hospital in Hanoi, and died on March 29, 2003, just a month after being called in to investigate.[3]

New Virus Quickly Identified

The global effort to identify the cause of SARS succeeded in a remarkably short time. On April 16, 2003, WHO announced that SARS was caused by a new strain of a type of virus called a coronavirus. Coronaviruses cause a variety of upper respiratory infections (including the

Infectious Disease Specialists

common cold) in humans. But where had this previously unknown strain come from?

Suspicion centered on the live animal markets of Guangdong, China, site of the first known human case. Most diseases that appear suddenly in humans are caused by viruses already circulating in animal populations that somehow make the leap from animals to humans.

WHO sent a team to Guangdong to test animals in the markets for the SARS coronavirus. The team tentatively concluded that the virus had jumped to humans from civets: small, catlike mammals native to the tropics of Africa and Asia. But although the strain of the virus they found in civets almost perfectly matched

An animal market in the Guangdong province of China sells wild animals as food. Scientists believed SARS had originated in the animals sold at one of these markets.

the virus isolated from the first human case, that did not necessarily mean civets were the natural reservoir, the animals the virus normally circulates among.

"As with any new disease, the tests are always less than perfect," Jonathan Epstein explains. "They had a bunch of spurious [false] positive results, not just civets, but a few other species—raccoondogs, ferret badgers,—so there wasn't any sort of hard and fast evidence."[4]

At the time, Epstein's research was focused on the Nipah virus, which emerged in Malaysia and killed a hundred people by the end of June 1999. The virus first attacked the respiratory system in pigs, but then jumped to humans, causing encephalitis—brain inflammation. Several more outbreaks have occurred in other parts of Asia since the virus was first identified. Researchers found that the virus's natural reservoir was bats, and that the virus had jumped from them to pigs to humans.

In Bangladesh, where there have been outbreaks reported nearly every year since 2001, people typically become infected by the Nipah virus by drinking date palm sap—a sugary drink collected from palm trees overnight. The sweet sap also attracts fruit bats that inadvertently contaminate the sap with saliva, urine, or other excreta as they lick the sap as it flows along the tree truck into collecting pots. It is an example of a deadly virus that accidentally spills over into people from bats via a man-made food source (date palm sap) that bats have learned to exploit.[5]

Infectious Disease Specialists

In Malaysia, Epstein studied *Pteropus vampyrus*, which is the largest bat species in the world. This species is one of two that carry the deadly Nipah virus.

Epstein and his colleagues were looking for research partners interested in testing bats in China for viruses related to the Nipah virus. With

JONATHAN EPSTEIN: SEEKING THE SOURCE OF SARS

An Expedition to China

Epstein led the first expedition. "There were scientists with expertise on a lot of things related to bat biology as well as virologists with laboratory expertise, but no one had a lot of experience collecting diagnostic samples from wild animals," he explains.

His main function was to lead the expedition in the wild and help catch and sample the bats. He talked to the members of the expedition about how to protect themselves from infectious diseases. He also showed expedition members how to safely catch the bats without harming them and release them again after samples had been collected.

When people think of bats, they think of caves. But in fact, bats live in all kinds of different environments, from caves to attics to forests to, yes, belfries. It largely depends on their diet. Fruit-eating bats tend to live in trees in the woods, while insect-eating bats tend to live in buildings or caves.

Most of the bats in China (and the world) are insect-eaters, Epstein says. In the part of China where the expedition took place there were extensive cave systems, with some caverns as large as airplane hangars. "Some of the species of bats that we were looking at were also the ones that are traded in the market for food, particularly bats of the genus *Rhinolophus*," he says. "We were hiking into these cave systems, some of them about two kilometers [one mile] long, looking for bat colonies we could sample and test."

Infectious Disease Specialists

To do so, they would string large "mist nets," similar to a volleyball net but with a much finer mesh, between two twenty-foot-tall (six meters) bamboo poles.

Normally the poles are raised and anchored and the net strung between them along a flyway the bats might travel through. But within the caves, there wasn't a lot of solid ground in which to anchor the poles. As well, the ceilings were so high the bats could simply have flown over the top of the nets.

Epstein collected samples from various bat species to see how they are involved in the spread of deadly diseases such as SARS.

JONATHAN EPSTEIN: SEEKING THE SOURCE OF SARS

"We were actually climbing up stalagmites and perching on top of some of these rocky outcroppings that were twenty feet off the ground, two of us, each of us holding a pole and stringing these nets up between us," Epstein says. The goal was to get the net close enough to the ceiling to catch the bats as they flew in.

In another case, the bats were roosting in a smaller cavern off the main cave. The only way into the smaller cavern was through a tunnel high up in the wall of the main cave. To get the nets into the smaller cavern, "we fashioned ladders, and we climbed up to this hole that was probably about twelve feet in diameter [and] forty feet off the ground," Epstein says.

Still, Epstein thought it an improvement from other expeditions he had been on. While looking for the Nipah virus in fruit bats living in mangrove swamps in Malaysia, he had to wade through five feet (1.5 meters) of water.

"Wherever you work with bats," Epstein says, "you have to work at night, and you're dealing with wild animals that are much more adapted to their environment than [humans] are."

Netting Bats

A lot of the challenge in working with bats is setting the nets in the right places and making sure that you know how the bats are going to fly, in which direction, and in what numbers. Assuming all the work has gone well, the bats end up unhurt but entangled in the mesh. Then

Infectious Disease Specialists

> ## ⚠ Bats in Brief
>
> **Bats are the only** mammals that have evolved true flight: the ability to fly by flapping their wings, as opposed to simply gliding. There are more than 1,200 species worldwide, ranging in size from the huge Malayan flying fox, which can have a wingspan of more than five feet, to the Philippine bamboo bat, whose wingspan is only slightly over half an inch.
>
> Various species eat small mammals, reptiles, birds, fish, other bats, fruit, flowers, nectar, pollen, leaves, and, in the case of the infamous vampire bat, blood.

you have to retrieve them without hurting them—or yourself.

Since the researchers believed that SARS could be transmitted by bats, they had to take precautions. Just inhaling dust from bat guano (feces) could have put the researchers at risk. To minimize that risk, the researchers wore long clothes, facemasks with filters, safety glasses, and, of course, gloves made of a tough material that is puncture-resistant but allows for normal movement. Wearing gloves is always a good idea when handling bats, because bats "have pretty sharp teeth," Epstein notes.

As each bat was untangled, it was put into a small cloth bag in which the bats could hang. That calmed them. When the bats were calm, the scientists began collecting samples of blood, saliva, and feces.

JONATHAN EPSTEIN: SEEKING THE SOURCE OF SARS

"We would set up a mobile field lab, generally just a table where we had very small needles and syringes and sterile swabs," Epstein says. In addition to collecting samples, they would measure the bat's body mass, length, and forearm length.

The researchers did their best not to harm the animals—although, Epstein notes, there is always some stress to an animal when you are catching and manually restraining it. "That's where some of my expertise as a veterinarian came in," he says, "being able to restrain

Epstein and colleagues from China and Australia descend into a cave where they will look for bats that may be carrying the SARS coronavirus.

> **Infectious Disease Specialists**

wild animals without hurting them or without getting hurt."

The Bats Test Positive

The samples were then taken back to the lab to be tested for the SARS coronavirus, and . . . eureka! The scientists discovered that between 30 and 40 percent of the bats from the *Rhinolophus* genus tested positive for antibodies for the SARS coronavirus, even though they were not sick and (obviously) not dead. "That suggests that the virus has spread through a good proportion of the population, and that those animals have survived infection with antibodies and are now resistant," Epstein explains.

Laboratories in China and Australia were also able to detect some of the virus's genetic material in the samples from the bats. The presence of antibodies proved that the bats had been exposed to the virus. The presence of genetic material proved that they were still carrying it.

The lab results revealed four or five different viruses within the bats, all within the SARS coronavirus family. "When you look at a family tree of these viruses, the virus that infected humans in the outbreak in 2002–2003 fit right inside," Epstein says. Dubbing the human viruses "SARS-like coronaviruses," the researchers realized they were close to solving the puzzle and that the emergence of SARS may have been due to bats being caught from the wild and brought into Guangdong and other similar marketplaces.

JONATHAN EPSTEIN: SEEKING THE SOURCE OF SARS

Epstein releases a fruit bat back into its cave. The samples he collected from this and other species were tested for SARS coronavirus.

The Missing Link

Those marketplaces, Epstein explained, are "a complete menagerie [zoo]. There are animals of all species, of all types, alive and dead, being kept together in very unhygienic [dirty] conditions. As soon as someone picks one out, they butcher it with bare hands right there on site, so there is plenty of opportunity for cross-infection to occur among different animals as well as in the person doing the butchering."

Putting all the pieces together, scientists presumed that bats infected with a SARS-like coronavirus were brought into the marketplace, where they came in contact with civets. In the civets, the virus mutated. It then jumped from civets to people, which is why the virus found in civets was so similar to the one found in people.

However, one piece of the puzzle still challenged them, Epstein says. "When laboratory animals were infected with the SARS-like coronaviruses (an important step to verifying that a particular virus or pathogen causes the disease being studied) they didn't seem to be able to infect them. The SARS coronavirus used a specific mechanism to infect human lung cells and cause disease. The bat viruses we found didn't seem to be able to use that mechanism and therefore it was unlikely that these actual viruses were responsible for the original outbreak."

The researchers hypothesized there must be a whole spectrum of genetically related, but slightly different, SARS-like viruses that occurred in *Rhinolophus* bats. Research over the next decade both by Epstein's team and many other groups revealed that there were indeed many viruses related to SARS, which are carried by many different species of bats in Asia, Europe, and Africa.

> "However, none of these viruses were closer to SARS than the ones we found. We continued to work with our partners in China to sample Rhinolophus bats over the years, and in 2014, ten years after we had first identified bats as the probable source of SARS, we found a coronavirus in bats so similar to SARS that it did use the same mechanism to infect cells as SARS. This was the missing link! And it confirmed our

JONATHAN EPSTEIN: SEEKING THE SOURCE OF SARS

Civets, which live primarily in southern Asia, were found to carry the SARS virus from bats to humans.

suspicion that there was a virus in bats that could have directly infected people (and civets) in the Guangdong markets. This discovery shows how important long-term studies can be to provide answers to challenging scientific questions."

In 2012 Epstein joined a team of colleagues from Columbia University and EcoHealth Alliance, which, at the invitation of the Saudi Ministry of Health, went to Saudi Arabia to investigate the source of this virus.

"We caught bats and tested various other animals. We ended up discovering genetic material identical to MERS coronavirus in an Egyptian tomb bat, and over the next two years also found that camels were the major carriers of this virus in Saudi Arabia. Other

Infectious Disease Specialists

> ❗ **Middle East Respiratory Syndrome**
>
> **In 2012 a new disease** emerged in Saudi Arabia. Called Middle East Respiratory Syndrome (MERS), it has caused severe respiratory illness in more than eighty people, primarily in the Arabian Peninsula. The MERS virus is different from SARS, but closely related to other coronaviruses found in bats.

research has similarly found camels to be infected in many parts of Africa and the Middle East. The MERS epidemic is still ongoing and while camels appear to be a source of infection for some cases, and others are infected by people who already have MERS, it remains unknown exactly how most people acquire the virus. It is also unknown whether bats transmit this virus to camels, or directly to people."

EcoHealth Alliance and Columbia University continue to study the epidemiology of this emerging disease in the Middle East.[6]

Why did SARS emerge when it did, when bats have presumably been carrying the virus—and have been brought into the Chinese marketplaces—for a long time?

"A lot of it has to do with just luck and probability," Epstein says. "Bats have been brought in for a long time. Some have been infected, some have not. The ones that are infected have to be able to infect other animals, and the virus has to change such that it can readily infect both another species and then people."

JONATHAN EPSTEIN: SEEKING THE SOURCE OF SARS

Understanding the process is important, Epstein says, because scientists fear that what happened with SARS could happen with avian influenza (bird flu). The virus's goal is to spread, and, with the right combination, it could one day be easily transmitted from person to person. For a virus, says Epstein, "It's no good if it just gets somebody sick and then they recover without transmitting it."

Extermination Not the Answer

Part of the mission of Epstein's employer, EcoHealth Alliance, is to point out that problems such as the emergence of the SARS virus arise from human behavior, not from anything the animals have done.

Human activities that create opportunities for diseases in animals to spill over into people are called "anthropogenic factors" by researchers. "Normally people and animals wouldn't interact if it weren't for these activities, like the cultivation of date palm sap in Bangladesh," Epstein explains.

Anthropogenic factors also include trade in wildlife (such as that within the Chinese markets), global travel, and industrialization or agricultural expansion. Expansion of farms into wildlife habitats, like a rain forest, increases the interaction between wild animals and humans and domestic animals (pets and livestock) more than ever before. This is why we are seeing more emerging diseases than we have previously, says Epstein.

Infectious Disease Specialists

But, Epstein says, "The knee-jerk reaction from the public may be 'Well, if these bats are carrying a disease that kills people, why not just get rid of the bats?' Our job is to say, 'No, these animals serve a very important function ecologically.'"

Epstein points out that insect-eating bats are important for pest control and fruit-eating bats are vital to many plants as pollinators and seed-dispersers. "You can't just eliminate them. One, you would lose those ecological services. Two, if you remove them from an ecosystem you never know what might move in to take their place. You create a vacuum, and something worse could come in that carries even worse diseases."

To deal with emerging diseases, Epstein says, we need to better understand how people and animals interact, not simply try to eliminate the animals carrying the diseases. "We need to recognize that human activities are what are causing these diseases to emerge. It's not the fault of the animals," he says.

The Human/Animal Connection

Studying the interaction of humans and animals comes naturally to Epstein. When he went to veterinary school he already knew he wanted to work with wildlife. He also had a strong interest in the conservation of wild species.

The school he attended, Tufts University in Massachusetts, had a fairly new program at the time that combined a doctorate in veterinary medicine with a master's degree in public health. Over the four years of his veterinary training, Epstein also took classes at the medical school with medical students interested in focusing on public health.

"In the course of [my study] I started to see that there was a very real connection between human health and animal health," Epstein says. "That particularly was apparent with infectious diseases, because there are so many diseases out there that came from animals . . . also, a lot of the emerging diseases we see come from animals."

Becoming a veterinary epidemiologist was a way to work with wildlife and focus on improving human health at the same time, a combination that appealed to Epstein.

"Veterinarians have worked in public health for a while, but in the past ten years there has been a real recognition that human health issues and animal health issues are linked," Epstein says. "What has been really fascinating is that traditional barriers between physicians who work in public health, veterinarians, and other scientists—including virologists and ecologists—are melting away. You see a lot more collaborative teams that include people from a whole lot of different disciplines."

It is work, he says, that he finds "very exciting" and "incredibly rewarding" . . . even when he is wading five feet deep in mangrove swamps in Malaysia or scaling slimy stalagmites in Chinese caves.

Appendix: Infectious Disease Specialists: Jobs at a Glance[1]

	EPIDEMIOLOGIST
Education Required	Bachelor of science degree in a biological science; master's degree in public health or epidemiology, many positions require PhD and postdoctoral research in epidemiology
Salary Range*	$42,560 - $111,080
	MICROBIOLOGIST
Education Required	Bachelor of science degree in microbiology or related science; master's degree or, preferably, PhD and postdoctoral research in microbiology
Salary Range	$38,820 - $121,060
	RESEARCH SCIENTIST
Education Required	Bachelor's degree in physics, math, or related field; master's degree; PhD and postdoctoral research for high-level positions
Salary Range	$42,830 - $149,310
	WILDLIFE BIOLOGIST
Education Required	Bachelor of science degree in biology or biological sciences; master's degree or PhD in biological sciences for high-level positions
Salary Range	$37,150 – $95,460
	BIOLOGY PROFESSOR
Education Required	Bachelor's degree in biology; master's degree or, preferably, PhD in biology, two to six years as a postdoctoral scholar is common
Salary Range	$45,000 to $148,000
	VETERINARIAN
Education Required	Bachelor's degree in biology, chemistry, or related field; PhD in veterinary medicine
Salary Range	$53,270 - $149,530

(1) Bureau of Labor Statistics, *Occupational Outlook Handbook, 2014–15 Edition*, May 2013, US Department of Labor, http://www.bls.gov/oes/current/oes_stru.htm.

*Salary figures will vary according to job specifications, geographic location, and market demands.

Chapter Notes

Chapter 1. Investigating Disease

1. L.H. Taylor, S.M. Latham, and M.E. Woolhouse, "Risk Factors for Human Disease Emergence," *Philosophical transactions of the Royal Society of London, Series B, Biological Sciences* 356, No. 1411, July 29, 2001, 983–989, http://www.citeulike.org/user/skumagai/article/2876956.

Chapter 2. Marta Guerra: Battling Ebola

1. Arthur Schoenstadt, "Ebola Treatment," *eMedTV*, last modified August 12, 2014, http://ebola.emedtv.com/ebola/ebola-treatment.html.
2. Telephone interview with Marta Guerra, October 10, 2007, and follow-up e-mail interview, February 2015. All quotes from Guerra come from these interviews.

Chapter 3. James Strong: Science in a Space Suit

1. Telephone interview with James Strong, September 24, 2007, and follow-up email interview, February 2015. All quotes from Strong come from these interviews.
2. Centers for Disease Control and Prevention, "Section IV—Laboratory Biosafety Level Criteria," accessed March 22, 2015, http://www.cdc.gov/biosafety/publications/bmbl5/BMBL5_sect_IV.pdf.

Chapter 4. Laurie Richardson: Stalking the Coral Killer

1. World Resources Institute, "Reefs at Risk Revisited Key Findings," accessed February 26, 2015, http://www.wri.org/sites/default/files/reefs_at_risk_key_findings.pdf.

Infectious Disease Specialists

2. Telephone interview with Laurie Richardson, September 12, 2007, and follow-up e-mail interview, February 2015. All quotes from Richardson come from these interviews.
3. "Focus on Metagenomics," *Nature Reviews Microbiology*, accessed February 26, 2015, http://www.nature.com/nrmicro/focus/metagenomics/index.html.
4. Bennett Daviss, "Growing Pains for Metabolomics," *The Scientist*, April 25, 2005, http://www.the-scientist.com/?articles.view/articleNo/16400/title/Growing-Pains-for-Metabolomics/.

Chapter 5. Jonathan Runstadler: The Biology of Bird Flu

1. US Fish and Wildlife Service, "Migratory Bird Management: Overview," accessed February 27, 2015, http://www.fws.gov/alaska/mbsp/mbm/introduction.htm.
2. World Health Organization, "Avian Influenza Fact Sheet," last modified March 2014, http://www.who.int/mediacentre/factsheets/avian_influenza/en/.
3. World Health Organization, "Cumulative Number of Confirmed Human Cases for Avian Influenza A(H5N1) reported to WHO, 2003-2015," last modified February 3, 2015, http://www.who.int/influenza/human_animal_interface/EN_GIP_20150106CumulativeNumberH5N1cases_corrected.pdf.
4. "Avian Influenza Fact Sheet."
5. Telephone interview with Jon Runstadler, September 28, 2007, and follow-up e-mail interview, February 2015. All quotes from Runstadler come from these interviews.

CHAPTER NOTES

Chapter 6. Lisa Fernando: An Outbreak of Marburg

1. Telephone interview with Lisa Fernando, September 26, 2007, and follow-up e-mail interview, February 2015. All quotes from Fernando come from these interviews.

Chapter 7. Jonathan Epstein: Seeking the Source of SARS

1. Brigg Reilley, Michel Van Herp, Dan Sermand, and Nicoletta Dentico, "SARS and Carlo Urbani," *New England Journal of Medicine* 348 (May 15, 2003): 1951-1952, http://www.nejm.org/doi/full/10.1056/NEJMp030080.
2. Centers for Disease Control and Prevention, "Frequently Asked Questions about SARS," last modified July 2, 2012, http://www.cdc.gov/sars/about/faq.html.
3. Reilly, Van Herp, Sermand, and Dentico.
4. Telephone interview with Jonathan Epstein, September 14, 2007, and follow-up e-mail interview, February 2015. All quotes from Epstein come from these interviews.
5. E-mail interview with Jonathan Epstein, February 2015.
6. Ibid.

Glossary

AIDS—A serious disease of the human immune system that is caused by an infection of HIV and is transmitted through bodily fluids.

algae—Microscopic plants or plantlike organisms.

antibodies—Substances produced by the body to fight off specific infections.

bacteria—Single-celled microscopic organisms, some of which can cause disease.

biosafety—The steps taken in a laboratory to protect researchers and the public from disease-causing agents.

ecology—The study of how living things interact with each other and their environment.

emerging disease—A disease that has just appeared or has suddenly become more widespread.

epidemiology—The study of how often diseases affect different groups of people or animals, and why.

genetics—The study of how traits are passed down from generation to generation.

HIV—Human Immunodeficiency Virus, the virus that causes AIDS.

influenza—A severe respiratory disease, caused by a virus. Commonly called "the flu."

isolation ward—A hospital room with special features designed to prevent the spread of infectious diseases from patients kept inside it.

malaria—A mosquito-transmitted disease caused by microscopic parasites that infect the red blood cells.

GLOSSARY

metabolomics—The systematic study of the unique chemical fingerprints that specific cellular processes leave behind.

metagenomics—The study of a collection of genetic material from a mixed community of organisms.

microbial—Related to microscopic organisms.

microbiology—The study of microscopic organisms.

mutant—The product of a mutation.

mutation—A sudden change in one or more heritable characteristics from those of the parent organism(s), caused by a change in a gene or a chromosome.

pandemic—A disease that occurs globally over a wide area and affects a high percentage of people or animals.

pathogen—Something (usually a virus or bacterium) that causes disease.

reservoir species—An animal species that can carry a pathogen without suffering from the disease.

virology—The study of viruses.

virus—Extremely tiny disease-causing agents that can only reproduce by infecting living cells.

zoonotic—A disease transmitted from animals to humans.

Further Reading

Books

Allman, Toney. *Infectious Disease Research*. San Diego: Referencepoint Press, 2011.

Hand, Carol. *Epidemiology: The Fight Against Pandemics*. Edina, Minn.: Essential Library, 2015.

Keyser, Amber. *Anatomy of a Pandemic*. Mankato, Minn.: Capstone Press, 2011.

Levitt, Alexandra. *Deadly Outbreaks: How Medical Detectives Save Lives Threatened by Killer Pandemics, Exotic Viruses, and Drug-Resistant Parasites*. New York: Skyhorse Publishing, 2013.

Wanjie, Anne. *The Basics of Microbes*. New York: Rosen, 2013.

Web Sites

teenshealth.org/teen/infections/bacterial_viral/ebola.html

Provides detailed information about the Ebola virus, how it is transmitted and treated.

diseasedetectives.org

Includes videos of real-life disease detectives at work.

Videos

Ebola Outbreak. Directed by Wael Dabbous. PBS Video, September 9, 2014. Running time 27:26.

video.pbs.org/video/2365321806/

Global Disease Detectives. Center for Disease Control and Prevention, 2011. Running time 6:41.

www.cdc.gov/globalhealth/video/gdd/diseasedetectives.htm

Index

A
algae, 52, 54, 63, 98
anthropogenic factors, 115–116
autoimmune deficiency syndrome (AIDS), 21
avian influenza (bird flu, H5N1), 69–71, 74, 78–79, 84, 115

B
backup buddy, 42
bacteria, 8, 14, 36, 51–52, 54, 61, 63–64, 85, 96
bats, 7, 99, 103–108, 110–114, 116
biologists, 8, 64–65, 80, 96
black band disease, 7, 10, 51–52, 54, 61–62
Brant geese, 72

C
Canadian Science Centre for Human and Animal Health, 85–86, 96
caves, 7, 99, 105–107, 117
Centers for Disease Control and Prevention (CDC), 15, 18–19, 28, 31
civets, 102–103, 112–113
containment levels, 36, 48
coral reefs, 7, 10, 51–52, 54, 64, 67. *See also* black band disease.
coronavirus, 101–102, 110–114. *See also* SARS

D
decompression sickness, 57, 59–60
decontamination, 37, 42, 47–48
diseases, emerging, 8, 10, 114, 116–117
disease survey, 59
disease transmission
    Ebola, 7, 13–15, 17–28, 30–32, 35, 37, 39, 86–87, 93, 95
    human activity in, 115–116
    MERS, 113–114
    reservoir species in, 39, 80, 103
    SARS, 99–117

E
Ebola virus, 7, 13–15, 17–28, 30–32, 35, 37, 39, 86–87, 93, 95
E. coli, 36
ecology, 65, 78
education. *See also* Appendix.
    of African locals, 20–21, 22–23

Infectious Disease Specialists

epidemiology, 8, 17
microbiology, 52, 54, 85, 96
veterinary epidemiology, 17, 99, 104, 117
virology, 35
volunteering, 20, 31, 75, 82
wildlife biology, 78
encephalitis, 37, 103
Epidemic Intelligence Service (EIS), 17–19
epidemiology
    education, 17, 117
    overview, 8, 24
    veterinary, 17, 99, 104
Epstein, Jonathan, 99–117

F

Feldmann, Heinz, 35, 87, 89, 96
Fernando, Lisa, 85–87, 89–93, 95–98
Field, Hume, 104
fieldwork
    African Ebola, 24–27, 30–32
    underwater, 54, 56–57, 59–67
    veterinary epidemiology, 104, 117
    wildlife biology, 64, 78, 84, 116–117

G

global warming, 63–64
guano, 108
Guerra, Marta, 15, 17–28, 30–32

H

High Efficiency Particulate (HEPA) filters, 95
Human Immunodeficiency Virus (HIV), 21, 22

I

influenza, 14, 69–71, 74, 78–80, 84, 100, 115

L

Level 1 laboratory, 36
Level 2 laboratory, 36, 46, 48
Level 3 laboratory, 37
Level 4 laboratory, 33, 37, 41. *See also* virology.
    decontamination, 41, 48
    described, 33, 36–37
    entering, 36–37, 41
    "space suits," 33, 35–37, 39, 41–42, 44, 46–49, 95
    working in, 33, 36–37, 41, 46, 48–49, 86–87, 96, 98
live-animal marketplaces, 104, 110–111, 114

INDEX

M

malaria, 24–25, 93
mammals, 74, 102, 108
Marburg hemorrhagic
    fever, 35, 37, 39, 85–87,
    89–93, 95–98
metabolomics, 64
metagenomics, 64
microbial mats, 52, 66
microbiology
    education, 52, 54, 85, 96
    fieldwork, 35, 51, 64–
      65, 117
    medical, 85
    salary, 67
    specimen collection,
      64–65
microorganisms, 36–37, 47,
    63, 65
Middle Eastern Respiratory Syndrome (MERS),
    113–114
mist nets, 74, 106
mobile laboratory, 89, 91

N

National Institutes of
    Health (NIH), 64–65
Nipah virus, 103–104, 107

O

Outbreak (1995), 15, 17–18,
    32, 97

P

pandemic, 70–71, 84, 100
parasites, 8
passports, 19
physiology, 65
potassium, 14, 28, 30
precautions
    bats, 108
    Level 4 lab, 46
    vaccinations, 19
    virology, 84, 93, 95

R

real-time polymerase chain
    reaction (RT-PCR),
    92–93
rebel insurgents, 7, 25–26,
    28
reservoir species, 39, 80,
    103
Richardson, Laurie, 51–52,
    54, 56–57, 59–67
risks
    accidents, 36, 103
    decompression sickness, 57, 59–60
    exposure, 47
    rebel insurgents, 7,
      25–26, 28
    underwater currents, 60
Rundstadler, Jonathan,
    71–72, 74–82, 84

Infectious Disease Specialists

S

safety
   decontamination, 37, 42, 47–48
   "space suits," 33, 35–37, 39, 41–42, 44, 46–49, 95
   underwater, 57, 59–61
salaries, 66–67. *See also* Appendix.
Sedinger, Jim, 72
specimen collection
   bats, 7, 99, 104–110
   microbiology, 64–65
   underwater, 54, 56–57, 59–61
   virology, 105
   wildlife biology, 72, 74–76, 99, 105–110
St. Mary's Hospital, 19, 28
Strong, James, 33, 35, 39, 41–42, 44, 46–49
Sudden Acute Respiratory Syndrome (SARS), 99–117

T

transect lines, 57, 59
tuberculosis, 37

V

vaccinations, 19
veterinarians, 8, 15, 17, 99, 109–110, 117
veterinary epidemiology
   education, 8, 17, 31, 99
   fieldwork, 117
   live-animal marketplaces, 104, 110–111, 114
   SARS, 104
virology
   education, 35
   fieldwork, 105
   precautions, 84, 93, 95
   specimen collection, 105
volunteers, 20, 31, 75, 82

W

weasels, 81
wildlife biology
   anthropogenic factors, 115–116
   education, 78
   fieldwork, 64, 78, 84, 116–117
   specimen collection, 72, 74–76, 99, 105–110
World Health Organization (WHO), 31, 87, 95, 100–102

Z

zoonotic diseases, 8, 17